rob&sara.com

ALSO AVAILABLE FROM
LAUREL-LEAF BOOKS

rob&
sara.
com

P. J. Petersen and Ivy Ruckman

Published by Laurel-Leaf
an imprint of Random House Children's Books
a division of Random House, Inc.
New York

Originally published in hardcover in the United States by Delacorte
Press, New York, in 2004. This edition published by arrangement
with Delacorte Press.

www.randomhouse.com/teens

Educators and librarians, for a variety of teaching tools, visit us at
www.randomhouse.com/teachers
RL: 6.0
ISBN-13: 978-0-440-23873-7
ISBN-10: 0-440-23873-0
July 2006
Printed in the United States of America
10 9 8 7 6 5 4 3 2 1

For Hillary Thalmann, Hannah Thalmann, Allie Ruckman, Ellis Ruckman, Ryan Harvey, and Emma Harvey.

And for each other.

rob&sara.com

BEFORE YOU START

A Word from Rob

This book wasn't my idea. I was against it at first. And I still feel funny about having my e-mail messages out where anybody with a library card can read them.

It was Sara's aunt Ginny who said we had a story to tell. And she'd had a college roommate who was now a New York editor.

Sara had saved every single e-mail, both mine and hers. So the story was all there. Along with pages and pages of day-to-day stuff that didn't matter.

DELETE TIME: Goodbye to class schedules, homework/music/weather talk, University High football and volleyball scores (pitiful—those teams should pay us for not telling). We also cut some of the boring "Sorry about your . . ." and "Glad to hear about your . . ." comments. And one dumb-blonde joke I sent to Sara. (Didn't make that mistake again.)

So you're not getting every word we wrote. But you won't be missing anything—unless you were on one of those teams that blasted University High.

While we were zapping all that stuff, I thought about cutting some of the places where I was really stupid. But I didn't. I figured "stupid" was part of the story.

⟨SEPTEMBER⟩

POETS 'N' WANNABES

A Bulletin Board for Teen Poets

The Sacrifice

My hair is gone!
My gorgeous, golden, strokeable hair—
it's gone! I'm shaved to the scalp
to make Angie feel better.
Five of us are look-alikes now,
indistinguishable from the rear but for
ears that protrude like naked
pink knobs.
I hope Angie gets through chemo.
I hope she feels better
now that we've all lost our hair.
I wish I did.

Submitted by Sara4348 <Thurs. Sept. 19 4:42PM>

POETS 'N' WANNABES

Instant Critique

Wesley: yeah, sintax—but
that first line sets up
the poem—it's the second
one (**GAG**) best to chop
it!

Sintax: golden and
gorjus???? Ok dude totally
clishay

Carol16: But doesn't that
let you know what a
disaster??? If she'd said
"my rats nest head of
stringy hair is gone" we'd
think "good riddance,
about time!!!"

Cattlecall: hey, you guys,
did four people get shaved
or five—do you count
Angie?—your confusin'
me, Sara

[8 in room]
Robcruise99
Cattlecall
MelodyV
Wesley
Sintax
Sara4348
Iambicpentup
Carol16

Wesley: CC, you bean-counter, what does it matter? Better try scanning that long line in the middle—sheesh! Talk about jarring rhythm!

Robcruise99: It's a good poem. I like it.

MelodyV: HUH? . . . YOU DO? I might like it but for the word choice—*naked pink knobs*—why a loaded word like *naked*??? And *protrude*? Ugly. So NOT a great image!

Robcruise99: I like it the way it is. Especially the ending.

Sintax: you go for naked, huh, and all that stroke-able hair??? (lol) having a little fantisy there, Rob?

Robcruise99: This is sick. I'm out of here.

Sent: Friday, September 20 4:28PM
From: Poets'n'wannabes@cyberwest.com
To: Sara4348@aol.com
Subj: "The Sacrifice"

The bulletin board doesn't print addresses, but I think they'll forward this to you. No big message. I just wanted to tell you that I like your poem. It's real, and it's honest. Forget those piranhas. They don't want poems. They just want victims.

If you feel like sending a poem or a comment to somebody who couldn't care less about "jarring rhythm," my address is Robcruise99@yahoo.com. Don't worry. I'm weird, but I'm not dangerous. And I won't send you spam.

Sent: Saturday, September 21 2:20PM
From: Sara4348@aol.com
To: Robcruise99@yahoo.com
Subj: Trashing Sara

Hi, Rob, if that's your name. Your email kept me from leaping off the chapel roof. Which I was considering. Not because my poem was treated like roadkill, but because nobody so much as mentioned cancer. What about content? Doesn't anybody care where a poem came from? Or what inspired it?

Anyway, thanks for liking "The Sacrifice"—and for saying so.

Sent: Sunday, September 22 4:08PM
From: Robcruise99@yahoo.com
To: Sara4348@aol.com
Subj: Question

One question, Sara-Four-Thousand-Three-Hundred-and-Forty-Eight. Did you really get your head shaved? I mean, you don't have to be dying to write a poem about a dying person. It's none of my business, but I'm curious. Are you really a skinhead?

Sent: Sunday, September 22 7:29PM
From: Sara4348@aol.com
To: Robcruise99@yahoo.com
Subj: An answer for "Curious"

Yes, for now I'm a skinhead. If I had a scanner, I'd send proof. And you may continue to call me that—*if* you don't value your front teeth.

You want the rest of the story? Three of us went straight to a picture booth at the mall after the barber's—all except Jessie, who was by then catatonic over what she'd done. We were scared to go home, so we cried our eyes out over a plate of hot potato skins first. (I was crying for Angie as much as myself. Her cancer is stage III and she's my best friend.)
—Sara

Sent: Monday, September 23 4:05PM
From: Robcruise99@yahoo.com
To: Sara4348@aol.com
Subj: Your poem
Sara—

Quick, check the bulletin board! Six more responses—all good. Okay, the one from ShebaQ is a little strange. But she

8

loved the poem—said so three times—even if she's "crying all over her keyboard."

None of your new fans (except ShebaQ) say much about the cancer. No surprise. It's hard to talk about without sounding dumb. I just wrote, "Angie's lucky to have friends like you." Then I deleted it. Angie, lucky? With cancer? See what I mean?

But congratulations! You and your friends are now my all-time favorite skinheads. You knocked my neighbor Roger out of the number-one spot. (Roger has a Confederate flag and an alligator tattooed on his bare scalp. Pretty smart for a skinhead. If he lets his hair grow, the tattoos disappear.)

I just checked the board again. Piranha time. When they start by calling your poem "charming," you know they're getting ready to rip out your liver. But the score is still 6–1. And it's still a good poem, no matter what some "wannabe" says.
—Weird Rob

Monday, September 23 8:10PM
From: Sara4348@aol.com
To: Robcruise99@yahoo.com
Subj: Thanks, but no thanks to any more BB

Rob—

I checked the critiques again and admit I felt slightly better—for about two minutes. Then I got to MelodyV's and Wesley's latest comments. They're still feasting on me. (They'd make a good pair, wouldn't they? Picture them reading Longfellow and Kipling by the fire—nothing jarring and, please, nothing naked.) You may be weird, Rob, but at least you're living in the real world, where kids mourn and go off and shave their heads.

Actually, you don't sound all that weird. And curious is good, unless you're a cat who loves tight places.

Guess what? I'm curious, too. And suddenly I'm thinking you must be a teacher-host . . . or you'd be trashing my poem like some of the others. (Teachers *have* to be supportive, you know? It's in their contracts.)

So write back and come clean. *Are* you one?

—Suspicious Sara

Sent: Tuesday, September 24 4:03PM
From: Robcruise99@yahoo.com
To: Sara4348@aol.com
Subj: Thanks for the laugh

Me—a teacher? That cracked me up.

You're sneaky, Sara. You start out by being nice, saying I don't sound so weird. Then you turn around and ask if I'm a teacher. You know how to hurt a guy.

Sent: Wednesday, September 25 4:04PM
From: Robcruise99@yahoo.com
To: Sara4348@aol.com
Subj: Another question

I just read your first e-mail again. You said I saved you from leaping off the chapel roof. Not a cliff or a bridge or a water tower. A chapel roof. Made me wonder. Do you go to one of those church schools? I can see it all now—you with your bald head in your blue-and-white uniform.

—Curious (Nosy) Rob

Sent: Wednesday, September 25 5:22PM
From: Sara4348@aol.com
To: Robcruise99@yahoo.com
Subj: Me-me-me talk

Hi, Rob!

Church school? No way. I live on a mellow old army post where my dad's the colonel. If you want to know where I'm from, I'm happy to give you the skinny: I'm from the military. I've lived all over the world.

But this year I'm lucky. I go to a regular school, even though I live on the post. The chapel roof happens to be the highest point above the parade ground. I've been up there, way up in the belfry. It's the perfect hideout. (But don't tell. Sometimes I don't want to be found.)

Good news! My scalp is starting to feel fuzzy. *Whoopeeeeeee!* I won't have to wear my Winter Olympics beret forever. Even better news—Angie gets her wig tomorrow. Jessie, our other friend, has done a full 180 and says she doesn't plan to cover up at all. She'd rather catch cold.

I keep trying to imagine who you are and what you look like. (Hope you're not bald.)

—Sara

Sent: Thursday, September 26 4:02PM
From: Robcruise99@yahoo.com
To: Sara4348@aol.com
Subj: Re: Me-me-me talk

You're getting to be my favorite poet. I really liked that line "Sometimes I don't want to be found." That's a whole poem in one sentence. I mean it. Take a look:

Sometimes
I
don't want
to
be
found.

See? It works. But don't feed it to the piranhas.

Sent: Friday, September 27 10:08PM
From: Sara4348@aol.com
To: Robcruise99@yahoo.com
Subj: A Friday slice of my life

I like what you did, turning my sentence into a poem. Nice! (Sure you're not a teacher?)

At dinner tonight I tried telling my folks I was writing to someone *très* interesting online. I got hit with so many questions, I stuck my fingers in my ears. (Not a well-thought-out move.) Dad, who wrote the manual on insubordination, got so mad he started to yell. I yelled back, "But you never listen!" Then he called me a smartmouth. In the end, Mom shushed us both and I stomped up to my room. I totally lost out on dessert: "Chocolate chunks crashing into creamy coffee ice cream." So much for sharing, huh?

Guess what happens a week from next Friday? I, Sara Whatzerface, am turning sixteen. I got my Utah permit six months ago, so now I'm up for the actual driving part. Dad says I'm scaring all the dogs on the post. (Verrrry funny!) But it's Mom who's missing bridge to drive with me. She'll be the one celebrating.

(Uh-oh, things are suddenly very quiet around here. Mom

and Dad must be asleep. Stand by . . . I'm gonna sneak downstairs and have a dish of that ice cream!)

—Sara

Sent: Saturday, September 28 4:02PM
From: Robcruise99@yahoo.com
To: Sara4348@aol.com
Subj: Driving

Okay, you get your license. You're free! Where do you go
first? (Besides Starbucks—for more of that ice cream.)

Sent: Saturday, September 28 8:37PM
From: Sara4348@aol.com
To: Robcruise99@yahoo.com
Subj: The Big Sixteen

What does it matter where I go first? Just picture me cruising anywhere I please. It's turning 16 that's THE BIGGIE. The
idea is this: as soon as I'm licensed, I can get a job. License
first, then wheels, then a job. Freedom, get it? Money! For
clothes I *like,* a pair of hot new skis, and more hours at the
climbing gym.

Am I boring you? You've probably been through all this
"turning sixteen" stuff. I bet you already have a car and a girlfriend who has hair.

I just looked back at your emails. You definitely strike me
as being older than guys I know at school. Are you in high
school? College? Out of school and working? (Wooooo, scary!
You could be a lurking pedophile or something.) Time to ask
questions.

Okay, so now it's your turn. My life's an open book. The
only thing I haven't mentioned is that I have a brother. Gabe's

away at college. I couldn't wait for him to leave home, but now I really do miss him.

Here's an assignment: Write an essay entitled "About Me" and turn it in on Friday. I'll play teacher and grade it.

Sent: Sunday, September 29 4:06PM
From: Robcruise99@yahoo.com
To: Sara4348@aol.com
Subj: My homework assignment

Come on, Sara. What makes you think I do homework? Besides, you don't want to hear about my life. Too boring.

Sent: Sunday, September 29 5:28PM
From: Sara4348@aol.com
To: Robcruise99@yahoo.com
Subj: Don't make me give you an F!

I do, I Do, I positively DO want to hear about your life! And doesn't everyone have to do homework? It's encoded in our DNA.

Besides, you'll never get to hear about my life if I don't get to hear about yours.

So get to work!

—Mean Sara

⟨OCTOBER⟩

Sent: Tuesday, October 1 4:01PM
From: Robcruise99@yahoo.com
To: Sara4348@aol.com
Subj: Okay, okay! ABOUT ME

Sara—

I can relate to how excited you are about getting a driver's license. That's how I felt last May when I got my pilot's license on my 16th birthday. I've been flying planes since I was twelve. My dream is to attend the U.S. Air Force Academy in Colorado Springs, and I'm doing all I can to make it happen.

And your first job—that's big. I started as a courtesy clerk at Safeway. I can't work after school right now. I have football practice, then homework. (I need A's to get into the Academy.) But I need money for flying lessons, so I get up at 4:30 every morning and deliver newspapers in my 1970 VW—not the kind of car I'd recommend unless you're a mechanic.

What else? I have two sisters and a brother, all younger. I like sports, especially basketball. I'd rather play than watch. I play the piano and the guitar. I'm not great, but I'm good enough to have fun.

That's probably more than you wanted to know. If I've left anything out, just ask.

Sent: Tuesday, October 1 4:02PM
From: Robcruise99@yahoo.com
To: Sara4348@aol.com
Subj: About me (again)

Sara—

Have you seen old bikers? Guys who look way too old to be out there on their Harleys? Bald guys, and ones with gray beards and wrinkled-up grandpa faces? That's my dad and his buddies. They always say, "We may get old, but we'll never grow up."

My dad and I live in a trailer park in the San Fernando Valley. Mom died when I was eight, so that kind of puts me in charge of the place. I do the shopping and cooking and cleaning. (Just don't inspect.)

Dad is laid-back, funny, and smart—a physics major at UCLA in the old days. He's more like a roommate than a father. I have no rules, can pretty much do anything I want. But don't start thinking "party time." I've seen too many drunks and dopers.

When I told Dad I needed a car, he said, "Great. Get a job and buy one." That's what I'm doing right now. I work after school and on weekends at a computer place. (No, I'm not a techie. I sweep floors and unpack boxes.)

I like movies and video games and pizza. I also like girls, but it's tough when you don't have a car. I like running, too. I've done some 10K races, hope to do a marathon someday.

So that's my life right now. I feel pretty lucky. Especially when I hear about someone like Angie.

Sent: Tuesday, October 1 4:03PM
From: Robcruise99@yahoo.com
To: Sara4348@aol.com
Subj: Take your pick

Hey, Teacher, do I get extra credit for doing two? Which Rob do you like? I also started one from a vampire and one from a Kansas farm kid who had a Hereford bull. But I got bored with those guys.

Besides, I made my point (I hope). I could be anybody. I'm just a guy out in cyberspace who liked your poem and who likes hearing from you. I'm weird, I guess, but I'd rather not talk much about my history or my day-to-day life. (One time through was enough. Who needs a replay?)

Is that all right, or are you going to thumb your nose and zap me out of your address book?

—Rob

PS If you haven't zapped me, tell me about Angie.

Sent: Tuesday, October 1 7:08PM
From: Sara4348@aol.com
To: Robcruise99@yahoo.com
Subj: Your assignment

HOLY KANSAS COW! You totally blew me away! Here's a big fat A+ for creativity/writing both. But now I'm more confused than ever. Am I supposed to choose my own Rob? Is that the idea?

To be honest, I wasn't crazy about the first profile. My face probably fell while I was reading it. That Rob is too stuck on himself. I half expected him to claim he was Tom Cruise's son. So . . . nix Rob #1.

I guess I envy Rob #2. I couldn't stand to lose my mom, but wow, all that great roommate stuff with his dad. How would it be, to be your own boss with no rules? Teenager heaven! I wonder, though. That second Rob sounds . . . well . . . too squared away, like the fiction he probably is. However, I'd rather go for a pizza with *him* than with #1.

The Rob I like most is the one who did the last email. He's no doubt some of each with a little vampire thrown in. Okay, so you may not want to write about your day-to-day life, but you'd better know that I'm a very daily kind of girl. I also have a history that is miles long and is just begging to be shared. So it's *you* who may want to zap me out of your address book.

Thanks for asking about Angie again. She looks adorable in her new wig and lets us all style it. The bad news is that the latest chemo is making her very sick, so they're starting over.

Sent: Thursday, October 3 4:02PM
From: Robcruise99@yahoo.com
To: Sara4348@aol.com
Subj: A message from your A student

"No doubt some of each"? OUCH! A little bit of vampire I can live with. Thanks for not adding a little bit of Kansas clod.

All that work and you didn't even like my guys. How could you not love that starry-eyed jock who gets up at 4:30 in the morning? I could hear violins playing when I wrote that.

You say you're a "very daily kind of girl." I'm not sure what that means, but I don't think I'm the daily kind. I'm more of a special-times guy. I get through the daily stuff by thinking about those times when everything was just right. Like the time I shared my breakfast with a coyote.

Thanks for the A. It's been a long time since I got one of those.

—Rob

Sent: Friday, October 4 3:37PM
From: Sara4348@aol.com
To: Robcruise99@yahoo.com
Subj: Your coyote story

DAILINESS GIRL MEETS SPECIAL-TIMES GUY

Makes a catchy headline. Let's talk about it sometime. Right now, though, I want to hear about the coyote. *Who? What? When? Where? Why?* (Can you tell I'm taking journalism?)

But how can I wait for a story like that? Want to do instant messaging? Let me know.

Sent: Friday, October 4 4:04PM
From: Robcruise99@yahoo.com
To: Sara4348@aol.com
Subj: GIWW (Good Idea—Won't Work)

Sorry, Sara. Instant messaging would be fun, but I can't do it on this system. I have my own laptop, but can't go online with it.

Here's how things work here: I get ten minutes a day on the school's big computer—the only one with an Internet connection. That's supposed to be time for downloading lessons. So unless I keep it short, I usually write my message to you ahead of time, save it on a disk, then e-mail it when I can. Confusing, huh? Maybe the suspense is good for us. Tell a joke, wait two days to see if you laugh.

Sent: Friday, October 4 9:51PM
From: Sara4348@aol.com
To: Robcruise99@yahoo.com
Subj: BAD NEWS!

Rob———!!!

Nothing's making me laugh right now. I'm grounded for a week. My parental Internet czars say I can't use the computer except for homework—part of my "sentence" this time. (Are they getting stricter now that Gabe's gone? Seems like it!)

Anyway, they're downstairs watching a game. I'm alone up here and taking a big chance writing by the light of my watch dial. But I decided writing you is worth it.

I'm really missing Gabe tonight. When he was home, he'd make a game out of punishment. He'd write these silly limericks and slide them under my door. (Sometimes with a stick of Doublemint.) They always started with "There was a young lady named Sara," then went straight downhill from there. He had no (I repeat, *no*) poetry genes.

He'll be calling me on my birthday come Friday. I made him promise.

Whoops, gotta go, game's over———

Sent: Saturday, October 5 4:01PM
From: Robcruise99@yahoo.com
To: Sara4348@aol.com
Subj: Re: BAD NEWS!

Grounded? What did you do, forget to salute the colonel? You could use a lesson in Zen nose-thumbing. You merely think the thumb and finger positions while keeping a perfectly straight face. The other guy, the thumbee, can't tell. Try it, it'll make you feel better.

Sent: Sunday, October 6 4:06PM
From: Robcruise99@yahoo.com
To: Sara4348@aol.com
Subj: Borrowing from Gabe

Hang on, Sara!

Your brother's probably busy at college, so I wrote his
poem for him.

There was a young lady named Sara
Who shaved off all of her hair-uh.
Her poor mother cried.
Her daddy first sighed
And then he began to swear-uh.

(Sorry I can't include a stick of Doublemint.)

Sent: Sunday, October 6 8:22PM
From: Sara4348@aol.com
To: Robcruise99@yahoo.com
Subj: Update from my dark little cell . . .

Thank you, thank you! Your poem was the only bright
spot in my weekend.

I've been working on one myself. "There was a young feller
named Rob—" That's as far as I got. I'm not as good as you.

I'm writing fast. Have to keep an ear out. I was grounded
because I "stole" (Dad's word) Mom's car and took Angie for
a smoothie. Was that stupid or what?

More later. Don't forget the coyote who came for breakfast.

—Sara

```
Sent: Monday, October 7 4:00PM
From: Robcruise99@yahoo.com
To: Sara4348@aol.com
Subj: Another poem from your brother
```

An angry young woman named Sara
Said, "If I wasn't so nice, I would swear-uh.
Took my friend for a ride,
And some smoothies we buyed.
Now I'm grounded, and it just isn't fair-uh."

```
Sent: Monday, October 7 4:06PM
From: Robcruise99@yahoo.com
To: Sara4348@aol.com
Subj: Tell me more
```

You can't stop now. Give me all the details about your life of crime.

How's this for a deal? If you tell me about stealing the car, I'll try to finish writing about my coyote. (Harder than I thought.)

Keep smiling. (It'll drive them crazy.)

```
Sent: Monday, October 7 5:47PM
From: Sara4348@aol.com
To: Robcruise99@yahoo.com
Subj: Not you, too!
```

What really bites is that word—*stealing*. How could you, Rob?

Back up, okay? And keep in mind that I've been driving the Camry accident-free for six months now. I am *not* a criminal.

When Angie didn't show at school Friday, I called to see why. She said she was feeling so rotten she couldn't swallow so much as a Cheerio. I asked what would taste good—if anything. She laughed (a nice sound) and said, "A tall raspberry smoothie."

"See you in five," I told her. Mom's car was in the driveway, she was at a tea with Angie's mom, and the 7-11 is less than a mile away. So I grabbed the keys, backed out s-l-o-w-l-y, and headed for Angie's on the other side of the parade ground. I didn't stop to process the whole thing, you know? I just did it.

Angie had a smoothie and slurped up every ounce. Me too, of course. Then we sat in the car awhile and laughed about the robot nurses at the chemo place. She calls them R2 and D2. To their faces!

I went right home afterward, hoping my folks were still gone, but guess who was waiting in the driveway, his arms across his chest? I'd hardly parked when Mom came out, too, giving me the your-brother-should-have-been-an-only-child look.

What could I say? Okay, so I broke the law a little. I told them about Angie and how she couldn't eat anything. I said I was sorry. But I wasn't—not deep down. And I'm still not. It was worth getting grounded to hear Angie giggling again.

I don't know where Mom's gone now, but if she catches me at this, I'll be walking the rest of my life. Hey, I liked that second limerick even better.

Question: Were you the coyote's breakfast? You promised me a story, remember?

—Sara

Sent: Tuesday, October 8 4:08PM
From: Robcruise99@yahoo.com
To: Sara4348@aol.com
Subj: Re: Not you, too!

A skinhead car thief—what's next? My mother warned me about girls like you. But you're right. It was worth getting grounded.

Coyote story soon.

Sent: Wednesday, October 9 4:03PM
From: Robcruise99@yahoo.com
To: Sara4348@aol.com
Subj: My coyote

Hey, Sara, writing this coyote story was hard. I've never zapped so many words in my life.

Maybe you've seen pictures of the Malibu area. Not the beach and the little road and the houses on stilts. I'm talking about the mountains behind all that. You see monster houses built on the tops of the ridges. But in between the ridges are steep, brushy canyons.

I used to camp in those canyons when I wanted to get away from everything. Had the place to myself. Just me and the animals. The only way I could get through the brush was to follow the deer trails. And I still had to do lots of crawling.

One time I set up camp and went out exploring. I came back and found my stuff ripped apart. A coyote (I could see his tracks) had smelled the cheese in my pack and had chewed through the nylon and leather to get it.

After that, I kept watching for him. I was sure he was out there watching me. I usually don't feed the animals, but sometimes at night I'd leave some cheese at the edge of my little circle. It was always gone the next day.

Then one morning I was cooking bacon. You know how good that smells. I guess the coyote thought so, too. I looked up from my backpacking stove and saw him about fifteen feet away. Hunched down, watching me. I held up a piece of bacon, and (I swear this is true) he let out a little whine. ("Please" in coyote talk, maybe.)

I tossed the bacon toward him, but I didn't throw it far enough. It landed about four feet in front of him. He looked at me, then at the bacon. And he whined again. Then he made a leap, grabbed the bacon, did a 180, and disappeared.

No Hollywood ending here. We didn't become friends, and he didn't save my life. I never saw him again.

But I can still picture him there, hunched down, watching me. And I can still hear that little whine.

Sent: Thursday, October 10 8:38PM
From: Sara4348@aol.com
To: Robcruise99@yahoo.com
Subj: Who needs Hollywood endings?

Hi, Rob—

I love the coyote story! In fact, I liked it so much I showed it to Jessie and Angie during school lunch at the cafeteria. I hadn't told them about you, so they were all excited. But then Jessie was so totally in my face about guys on the Internet, I was sorry. (But Angie said, "Anyone who can befriend one of those scrawny, scabby coyotes is a friend of mine.") All the same, I made them vow they wouldn't tell *anyone*— exclamation point. So from now on you are my best-kept secret.

I take it you live in CA. In Malibu? In a big house on a ridge or in between? The canyons you describe—yikes! I'm picturing branches snapping in your face, stickery brush grabbing at your legs. I'd be terrified sleeping out there by myself and waking up eye-to-eye with a coyote. But thanks again for all the hard work of zapping and rewriting. Maybe you can hand it in for another A.

—Sara

P.S. It worked, the bit of "coyote talk" I borrowed from your story. "Please?" I begged my dad, with a little whine thrown in. It got me out of house arrest a day early, in time to take the driving test tomorrow. So I owe you.

Wish me luck. Sara again

```
Sent: Friday, October 11 9:49PM
From: Sara4348@aol.com
To: Robcruise99@yahoo.com
Subj: TOTAL MISERY!!!!!!!!!!!!!!!!!!!!!!!!!!!!!!!!!!
```

TURNING SIXTEEN SUCKS! I never want to do it again.

To start with (worst-case scenario come true), I flunked the driving test! I mean, I, Sara, who was born to take the wheel, smacked bumpers with the car behind as I was trying to parallel park. I nearly died. The officer himself felt bad, thinking I had cancer, no doubt, from my lack of hair. He explained that what I did was like an Olympic skier missing one of the gates—not terrible, but enough to shave off the points. (Yeah, yeah, yeah!)

I still can't believe it happened. I sulked all the way home—with my silent mother driving. How could I tell Angie? Or my brother, who would turn it into one of his dumb-blonde jokes? For once, after so much overseas duty, *we are a two-car family,* and I can't drive either one of them!

I needn't have worried about Gabe. He never called. Is this a stellar birthday or what?!

It's nearly bedtime now and I've been going through my closet looking for shoelaces. If I find enough, I may hang myself.

—Dejected Sara

Sent: Friday, October 11 8:49PM
From: DamianXXXX@yahoo.com
To: Sara4348@aol.com
Subj: (No subject)

R. SAYS HAPPY BIRTHDAY.

Sent: Friday, October 11 10:06PM
From: Sara4348@aol.com
To: Robcruise99@yahoo.com
Subj: Thank you, thank you!

Your "happy birthday" arrived with a *bing,* just as I was clicking SEND. We nearly had a head-on in cyberspace. How cool is that? Ahhhhh, relief! Someone remembered. Now I won't have to hang myself.

But who's the sender? I loved the greeting, but the rest is a trifle, um, mysterious. DamianXXXX@yahoo.com. Is that your new screen name? Better tell me, it nearly got deleted.

—Sara

```
Sent: Monday, October 14 6:47AM
From: Sara4348@aol.com
To: Robcruise99@yahoo.com
Subj: ??????????
```
Rob—is something wrong? Have I been too whiney?

```
Sent: Wednesday, October 16 7:10AM
From: Sara4348@aol.com
To: DamianXXXX@yahoo.com
Subj: A request
```
    Please tell me if Rob is okay. If Rob and Damian are one and the same, let me know.

—Sara4348, worried and wondering

```
Sent: Thursday, October 17 8:46PM
From: DamianXXXX@yahoo.com
To: Sara4348@aol.com
Subj: (No subject)
```
    R. SAYS WATE TILL FRIDAY.

```
Sent: Friday, October 18 4:00PM
From: Robcruise99@yahoo.com
To: Sara4348@aol.com
Subj: I'm back.
```
    Sorry you got worried. And sorry to be gone so long. I lost my Internet privileges for a week. I paid a kid to send you a birthday note. I had to write out "happy birthday." He couldn't spell either word. I have three messages from you (yaaay!) but only one minute left online. I'll download and read everything later. I'll explain tomorrow. Rob

Sent: Saturday, October 19 4:05PM
From: Robcruise99@yahoo.com
To: Sara4348@aol.com
Subj: Rotten times

Hey, Sara, maybe all the planets were in the wrong places last week. A girl here, an astrology nut, always blames bad times on the planets (Saturn's moon in Jupiter's orbit or something like that). Makes a neat excuse. It wasn't my fault—it was those planets.

No excuses here. Except bad timing. The same night I sent you the piece about the coyote, I was lying in bed and heard a coyote howl. Hadn't heard one for months. I was already feeling mad and closed in, and he starts hollering. I just had to get a look at him. I grabbed some stuff and sneaked out.

I knew it was stupid. I knew I'd get in trouble. But right then I didn't care.

I spent the night wandering around the hills. I found some tracks and heard the coyotes yapping, but I never saw them. (I have a feeling they saw me.)

I should have gone back to the school at daylight. That's what I've done before. But I couldn't stand to. So I stayed out the next day and night. When I finally went back, everybody was upset. (Big surprise.) I lied big-time—said I went for a walk Wednesday night and got lost. I don't think anybody believed that, but it gave them an easy out—they didn't have to list me as an official runaway. I lost all my privileges for a week and am on probation for three months.

So now, after a lo-o-ong week, I'm back online. Except that I only have five minutes a day of Internet time instead of the usual ten. Part of "the consequences of my action." But it's not a big problem. In five minutes I can take care of my school stuff and download the latest message from my favorite poet. Mainly, it means I can't answer right away.

Enough about me. What's happening there in Utah? I hope you get to take the driving test again right away. Then you and Angie can hop in the Camry, grab some tall raspberry smoothies, and blast out of there.

—Rob

Sent: Sunday, October 20 11:43AM
From: Sara4348@aol.com
To: Robcruise99@yahoo.com
Subj: *Where? When? Why?*

Rob—I was so relieved to get your email that I'm skipping church to answer. Did you honestly *do* that? Omigosh! What did you eat? Where did you sleep? Weren't you scared? Now you've come back to a grounding that makes mine look like movies with popcorn. I'm totally devastated.

I have no idea where you are, but right now I'm feeling you're very far away—like in a Cambodian school for monks. Or in Afghanistan, doing basic training. Or in Yosemite, sharing your laptop with a ledge full of hairy rock climbers. (You'd hear coyotes yipping if you were bivouacking on The Nose.)

See what happens? My imagination goes berserk. Please—a few more details. I really want to know. Where *exactly* are you?

Your Concerned Friend, Sara

Sent: Sunday, October 20 4:01PM
From: Robcruise99@yahoo.com
To: Sara4348@aol.com
Subj: Re: *Where? When? Why?*

Sara—

Where am I? Your imagination beats the heck out of reality. No Cambodian monastery. No Yosemite bivouac. I'm in a crummy little institution in Northern California. Details tomorrow.

—Rob

P.S. I ate some candy bars and slept on the ground. Was I scared? Nah. I'm safer sleeping in the hills than here.

Sent: Monday, October 21 4:01PM
From: Robcruise99@yahoo.com
To: Sara4348@aol.com
Subj: Where I Am

Okay, here's the story. I wish things were half as interesting here as the stuff you imagined.

I'm a resident of Pine Creek Academy. (That's the term they use—not *student* or *inmate*.) PCA is a boarding school that's kind of like a prison farm. No bars on the windows, but we're cut off from the outside world. We're in the mountains, ten miles from the nearest store. No phone calls or mail (except from parents), no live TV (movies and programs on tape). We wear uniforms. Jeans and Pine Creek T-shirts or sweatshirts. Blue for the girls, gray for the guys. (With these people, sometimes the color helps.) No jewelry, except for the cheap watches they give us. (Picture all those empty holes in the ears, noses, navels, etc.)

We're a weird bunch—deadeyes, reets, homefries, aliens, pit bulls, and skinheads (none of the help-Angie variety). My

33

friend Shannon calls us SIRs—Society's Irritating (or Immature) Rejects.

The number one thing here is *structure*. Everything planned. Everything by the clock. Control-freak school. No regular classrooms. Everybody has an individual program (mostly Internet lessons) and a daily schedule—with daily progress reports. I work in a room with a resources specialist and about fifteen other residents, each of us with a laptop.

The head guy, Dr. Fielding (everybody calls him Dr. Feelgood), says, "This is a boot camp, run by nice people. We're getting you in shape for life." If you cooperate (their favorite word), you earn privileges. If you go chasing coyotes, you lose them.

With the people here, anything can happen. Today at lunch Bethany, one of the homefries, went ballistic, jumped up onto the table, and ran up and down screaming. Bad trip or maybe a flashback. No damage done, except that she put her big blue Nike right in my macaroni.

So that's where I am. By now you're probably thinking that Jessie was right. Wasn't she the one who warned you about getting hooked up on the Internet with some weird guy?

—Weird (but still harmless) SIR Rob

Sent: Thursday, October 24 4:02PM
From: Robcruise99@yahoo.com
To: Sara4348@aol.com
Subj: A poem for you

> *A Utah girl named Sara*
> *Asked, "Rob, you live where-uh?"*
> *When he told her the facts,*
> *She gave him the axe*
> *And vanished into thin air-uh.*

Sent: Thursday, October 24 7:24PM
From: Sara4348@aol.com
To: Robcruise99@yahoo.com
Subj: Love your poem!

Rob—

I didn't vanish, not for long. Test week. I've been totally swamped, and I have a cold. No, wait . . . start over. That was a lie. I did have two tests and I *do* have a cold, but I could have found time.

I guess the idea of your being in an *institution* gave me a case of the chills. If your emails had come from a real prison, well, maybe things would be different. But here I am, back to writing SIR Rob, who lives, he says, among a society of rejects. It took me a while to sort out what that might mean.

I know I ask too many questions, but right now I have to, so put up with me, okay? I've never heard of reets or homefries or deadeyes. Are those gangs? It's obvious to me that you're not one of *them,* so what are you doing there? Everything I know about you (not a lot) tells me you're neither irritating nor immature, no matter how Shannon categorizes the residents. I'd say a little coyote escapade establishes your sanity, not the opposite!

The truth is, I couldn't bear to go back to the way things were before you read my poem. Maybe it doesn't matter who you are or aren't, or what Jessie might say. Maybe what matters is that you're as unanchored as I feel much of the time. Anyway, what can it hurt to reach out into the cyberfog and grab hands? I'll hang on if you will.

—Sara

Sent: Friday, October 25 4:04PM
From: Robcruise99@yahoo.com
To: Sara4348@aol.com
Subj: (No subject)

I only have two online minutes left, but I can't stand to wait a day to answer. It was great to hear from you. I was afraid you were gone. Reaching out into the cyberfog and grabbing hands—I love the idea.

—Rob

Sent: Saturday, October 26 4:02PM
From: Robcruise99@yahoo.com
To: Sara4348@aol.com
Subj: My "home"

So you got a case of the chills thinking about me here at Pine Creek Academy? Too much imagination, Sara.

I feel dumb telling you how unscary this place is. You're probably picturing concrete walls and uniformed guards. Nah! Think of log buildings in the pines, rock fireplaces, redwood window boxes full of flowers. Think picturesque.

They call this place a prep school, but the ads for it give you a different picture: IS YOUR CHILD ANGRY, TROUBLED, OUT OF CONTROL? My friend Shannon says this is an obedience school for kids—a place to send them if you can't train them at home.

Pine Creek is a kind of dumping ground. If you have a kid you can't stand, bring him here. No more worries, no more guilt.

He'll do better in a new environment, and you won't have a kid messing up your life. Another plus—you can now brag to your friends that Johnny is going to prep school.

Most of the people are brought here kicking and screaming. Not me. It was here or jail, so this looked pretty good. You may not think I'm irritating and immature (thanks, pal), but a lot of other people did. And they had good reasons.

I've been here since June. I live here 24/7 with the deadeyes (ones who've fried their brains with drugs) and the homefries (ones who are trying to do that) and the skinheads and all the rest—including us aliens.

A homefry story for you: These guys will try anything to get high—smoke anything, drink anything, inhale anything. No aerosol cans allowed here—for good reason. Last month a girl who was mad at them left a bottle of unlabeled pills in the bathroom. The pills were laxatives. You can guess the rest.

I hate it here, of course. I have 569 days before I turn 18 and go flying out the door. But I've been in worse places. Here, I have a room of my own and a laptop. We have a library, a gym, and pretty good food. We have lots of stupid rules, lots of messed-up people—but, hey, that's the world.

If you want to feel sorry for somebody, go for Angie. I'm doing all right.

—Rob

Sent: Sunday, October 27 10:30AM
From: Sara4348@aol.com
To: Robcruise99@yahoo.com
Subj: Prep school???????!!!!!!!!!!!!!!

So what *did* you do to get everyone on your case? First I was picturing you as a car thief in detention. (My crime of choice.) In the next frame, you were vandalizing one of those poshy Malibu mansions. All that institution talk, when all along you've been in that lovely prep school toasting marshmallows in a rock fireplace.

Sara, shut up! There's nothing funny about confinement in a wilderness detention camp. I'd hate it, too. And 568 days (one down) are way too many. I understand now why you didn't want to talk about your day-to-day life, but it's fine with me if you do. I'll just assume that you're one of the kids they advertise for—you're angry, troubled, out of control, or all-the-above. (Sounds like a profile of Sara, 16, army brat.)

Angie would kill me (kill us both) if she saw the last line of your email about who to feel sorry for. You wouldn't believe how tough she is. Always has been! (I've known her since Fort Bragg when we were both eight.) Even so, I happen to know she cries sometimes.

Better run. She and her folks are having brunch with us at the Officers' Club today. (Her dad's a major. Our moms are best friends.) Our dads want to talk about the latest rumors—the post being reactivated, possible transfers. Mom doesn't think it will happen. I hope she's right. I couldn't stand another move.
—Sara

Sent: Monday, October 28 4:01PM
From: Robcruise99@yahoo.com
To: Sara4348@aol.com
Subj: Greetings from Camp Feelgood

Here's the latest from "prep school." Today somebody got hold of the new brochure for this place. Beautiful pictures. Great sales pitch. Sweet-faced kid smiling up at a flag. The only thing is—the kid isn't one of us. He's some model they hired. Typical.

It's hard to give you a true picture of this place. I know it sounds like a freak show. And it is, in a way. We have guys who can't read, people so burned out on drugs that they drool on themselves, a wing full of hypers who can't sit still for two minutes. But we also have some smart people. And talented people—good musicians, good artists. Also moaners and whiners—and a little bunch who carry Bibles wherever they go.

Here's your test for today: What's the one thing all of us here at Pine Creek—skinheads, hypers, stoners, aliens, coyote chasers—have in common? (Skip the obvious answers like we're all weird or we all wish we were somewhere else.) Can you guess?

So maybe you'll be moving? I wish it was me.

—Rob

Sent: Tuesday, October 29 6:35PM
From: Sara4348@aol.com
To: Robcruise99@yahoo.com
Subj: The Quiz

Okay, I have a quiz to take: What do Rob and his classmates have in common? My first guess is Ritalin. (No, just kidding!) I would have guessed the obvious, that you all hate that place and wish you could bust out of there. The answer may be that you were all PUT there—for your own protection or society's. (See "Bethany and the Mashed Macaroni.") Am I close?

I've been trying to compare your place to the school I attend. No use. There's no comparison. Camp Feelgood is definitely more diverse (more interesting?) than where I go. Living there since June, you must have developed some tight friendships. The opposite, too, in the case of rotten kids you can't stand.

University High is sometimes called a prep school, too. You have to have grades to get in, which means we're a more homogeneous bunch. The emphasis is on academics. UH is more artsy than, say, career oriented. No auto shop, for instance. This school is lots more fun than the Department of Defense (DOD) schools that I've gone to overseas.

Anyway, I'm glad you gave yourself a separate category in yesterday's email. Coyote chaser is something I can understand. I have a hard time imagining the rest of Camp Feelgood's burned-out, cast-off student body.

Happy Halloween soon! I won't need a mask, scary as I look.

—Sara

Sent: Thursday, October 31 4:01PM
From: Robcruise99@yahoo.com
To: Sara4348@aol.com
Subj: Happy Halloween yourself!

You get a C+ on the quiz. You were wrong, but you made good guesses. The answer is simple—everybody here is rich. They have rich parents, anyway. This place costs more than Harvard or Yale, and they don't give scholarships.

You should get extra credit for the Ritalin guess. That's a big item here. Lots of residents get a daily dose. They have to take it in front of the eagle-eye nurse. If they can hide a pill under their tongues, they spit it out later and sell it to the homefries.

All these rich kids—it's a real shock when they find out you can't have money here. Just a little in our accounts so we can charge things like snacks and toothpaste at the school store. So people are always trying to figure out ways to sneak in cash (or drugs).

Dr. Feelgood and his staff do all they can. No mail except from parents. If you leave for a weekend or a vacation, you and your luggage get searched when you come back. And we have "bomb threats," which means the security people have to search everybody's room. Even so, most people (including me) have some money stashed. And the homefries always seem to find drugs somewhere. One guy had somebody from outside taping envelopes to the bumper of the garbage truck.

Enough about PCA. We're "definitely more diverse." (I love the way you put things.)

Hey, Sara, you're keeping secrets from me. Shannon told our group there's a fantastic new poem by Sara4348 on the P&W bulletin board. Shannon—Mlee1830 on the board—is the one who got me to that site in the first place. I went there to read a poem of hers and saw yours. (She doesn't know that I e-mail you.)

Do me a favor, okay? I'm still on shortened Internet sessions. You know how slow that board is. I could spend my whole five minutes signing in. What about sending me your poem directly? I promise not to point out the ugly words or jarring rhythm.

No parties here tonight. With this crew, every day is Halloween.

Sent: Thursday, October 31 5:48PM
From: Sara4348@aol.com
To: Robcruise99@yahoo.com
Subj: Poetry swap

You get my poem on one condition: You send me something of yours. Limericks accepted. *Promise before you download or sneak peeks at mine. Otherwise, the poetry virus will liquefy your hard drive.*

So Shannon is Mlee1830! No kidding? I've seen some of her poems, but didn't pay a lot of attention.

I'll send the poem after dinner. I have to check the chili and make salad. Chili, tossed salad, pumpkin pie—our traditional night-of-spooks meal, wherever we are in the world. (I've had to miss REAL Halloweens most of my life, Rob, so I love this whole trick-or-treat business. I'd go out myself if I thought I could get away with it.)

Whup, there's the doorbell. Unicorns are arriving already!

Sent: Thursday, October 31 9:33PM
From: Sara4348@aol.com
To: Robcruise99@yahoo.com
Subj: Remember . . . you asked for it!

Mistaking Identity

You think you see me, but you don't.
Those are merely arms and legs,
appendages sticking out from the book that hides my face.
The "I" you're looking for is in a cashew grove
in Mozambique
harvesting nuts for five cents an hour.

You think you've spotted me in Mexico,
there in the Square
Sipping choc'lat in my fine gauzy dress.
Guess again. I'm the girl with the dirty hands
selling Chiclets for a penny each.

How can you know me
when my shadow won't sit still?
When it jumps around on puppet strings?
When who I am depends so much on
where I am and what I see
and who touches my heart?

Pin me down? No way,
any more than I can you.

⟨NOVEMBER⟩

Sent: Saturday, November 2 4:01PM
From: Robcruise99@yahoo.com
To: Sara4348@aol.com
Subj: Your poem

Wow! (How's that for a deep comment?) But wow! I really like your poem. That first line is a poem all by itself:

> *You think*
> *you*
> *see me,*
> *but*
> *you*
> *don't.*

Or maybe—

> *You think you see me,*
>   *but*
>   *you*
>   *don't.*

I feel dumb telling you this, but you got me with your title. I read it and thought, "Oh, she's got the wrong word. She means *mistaken identity*." I read the poem about four times, and it suddenly hit me that I had fallen into the trap—seeing things wrong (again).

Wow! What else can I say? Okay, I owe you a poem or something. I wish I had one half that good (or even a quarter that good) to send back. Right now I'd feel stupid sending you another "There was a young lady named Sara" poem. Give me a few days.

—Rob

Sent: Saturday, November 2 6:47PM
From: Sara4348@aol.com
To: Robcruise99@yahoo.com
Subj: I'm blushing!

Thank you, thank you! You certainly know how to make a poet feel . . . well . . . *poetical*! Now I'll be looking for yours.

Yesterday, after doing seven perfect parallel parkings in a row, I thought of something cool we might do. What if we allow each other two tacked-on questions per email? We could call it *PSing*. (No resemblance to *BSing*, mind you.) We answer one question and ignore the other. What do you think? You can always change the rules and answer both . . . or none. (Keep it loose and easy. All we need in our lives is more structure, right?)

So . . . in the event you agree . . . here goes PSing, the first two.

1. Why don't you use "smilies," "frownies," and "winkies" or even *sound* like most teens on the Net? (I mean, Rob, we're *both* email weirdos. We actually use punctuation.)

2. Do you have parents somewhere?

Have to rush. We girls in "The Baldie Club" are going to watch Jessie play volleyball tonight. Movie after. "To celebrate that I'm still alive," Angie says. She's incredible. If only she could defeat this thing and have her whole long life to look forward to. We care so much—all of us—but we can't begin to know how it is.

—Sara

Sent: Monday, November 4 4:02PM
From: Robcruise99@yahoo.com
To: Sara4348@aol.com
Subj: Questions

Hey, Sara, I see how you operate. You ask two questions, but one of them is so dumb I really don't have a choice. Sneaky.

Can't you just see me using all that cutesy junk? :-J (said with tongue in cheek). How about @>—>— (offering you a rose)? Or maybe O:-) (what an angel!) You know what I think of all this? :-b (sticking my tongue out)

I don't have to answer the other question, but I will. Yeah, I have parents—Dr. Frankenstein and Mrs. Think Positive. He's a plastic surgeon who's had four wives (my mother was number three) and about a thousand girlfriends. My mother calls herself a recovering alcoholic—which means she doesn't drink. I hope that's true, but I wouldn't bet money on it. They're both disappointed with me. He tells me that (often), but she never would. What kind of cutesy mark would I use here? Maybe :/) (it's not funny).

Tell Angie hello from the Coyote Chaser.

No, I haven't forgotten about the poem I owe you.

—Rob

Sent: Monday, November 4 8:08PM
From: Sara4348@aol.com
To: Robcruise99@yahoo.com
Subj: Your email

Rob—

I'm starting to understand why you're at that academy. I guess you don't really have a home right now—or, at least, a family who can make a home for you.

Maybe that's why you seem older to me, because you *are* older when it comes to certain experiences. I can't imagine how I'd feel if my parents parked me somewhere and turned their backs.

I know, go ahead and remind me—I rag at my folks all the time. But they still love me. And I love them. I'd say they love each other, too, most of the time, but we never talk about stuff like that. They're kind of old-fashioned, know what I mean? And love is one of those subjects—like sex or prayer or Dad's paycheck—that never comes up at the dinner table.

Now, of course, I want to ask a zillion more questions, but maybe you'll tell me how you grew up to be *who you are* in spite of your parents' mountainous problems. But I won't use one of my PSes for asking.

—Sara

Sent: Tuesday, November 5 4:09PM
From: Robcruise99@yahoo.com
To: Sara4348@aol.com
Subj: Tuesday night

Hey, Sara, quit feeling sorry for me. I can't stand that. My folks didn't park me here and turn their backs. I did this to myself. I stole a car. (You and me, Sara.) A BMW convertible. If I didn't have a rich father with lots of connections, I'd be stuck in some juvenile detention facility right now. So I'm lucky to be here. Pine Creek is weird, but it beats jail.

Don't try to make me some pitiful little victim. Remember my coyote chasing? I knew I'd get in trouble, but I did it anyway. I've been doing stuff like that for years. A social worker told me, "The bottom line is that you're very stubborn and a little stupid." That's about it. I suffer from Stubborn-and-Stupid Disorder—ever heard of it?

I think there's a cutesy sign for NO CRYBABIES, but I don't know what it is. I'd use it here if I did.

Sent: Tuesday, November 5 7:22PM
From: Sara4348@aol.com
To: Robcruise99@yahoo.com
Subj: Hey, good taste in cars!

For now I'm going to ignore your crybaby remarks. But I can't ignore the rest. You stole a BMW? What were you thinking? That doesn't sound like the Rob I've been emailing. Come on, bud, you can't just drop something like that on me and then stop.

You telling this story for its shock value, or is it true? Details. I shared *my* "car theft," didn't I?
—Sara

Sent: Wednesday, November 6 4:09PM
From: Robcruise99@yahoo.com
To: Sara4348@aol.com
Subj: Stealing a BMW

You're right, Sara. You deserve the details.

Last spring I sneaked out of school because I couldn't stand to be there another minute. But the school security officer saw me. He called the police, then started chasing me, blowing his whistle. There I was—running down the street with a whistle-blower after me, and I could hear sirens getting close. I saw this BMW double-parked, engine running, outside a flower shop. I jumped in and took off. Racing through the city, running red lights, I could see the police cars behind me. I figured my only chance was to duck down an alley, so I— Nah! No way, Sara. (But how was that for "shock value"?)

The real truth: I did sneak out of a school, but nobody

saw me. I walked for hours, trying to get out of the city. Then I saw the double-parked car. It was a BMW, but I would have been just as happy with a cement truck. I just wanted to get out of there. I drove the car out into the country, locked it (even put up the top), and took off into the hills.

So that's my story. Not very exciting. But really stupid. Won myself a free trip to Camp Feelgood. I don't know what else to tell you. You see why I didn't want to start digging up the past?
—Rob

Sent: Wednesday, November 6 7:29PM
From: Sara4348@aol.com
To: Robcruise99@yahoo.com
Subj: (No subject)

Rob—

Wow! I can't believe you did that and you even put up the top? Crazy!

But all that stuff is history now, right? It looks as if you've learned some lessons—the hard way. Maybe it's time to move on.

Here are your questions for today. 1) What do you see outside your bedroom window? 2) Is Shannon your best friend, or is she your girlfriend?
—Sara

Sent: Thursday, November 7 4:19PM
From: Robcruise99@yahoo.com
To: Sara4348@aol.com
Subj: PS answers for Sara

Good idea, Sara. No more history. (I have ten extra minutes today—a little bribery—so I'll try to answer your questions.)

Shannon and I are buds, but that's nothing special. She's buds with all the aliens. She may be the smartest person here. Including all the teachers and doctors. Reads incredibly fast and remembers everything. She's funny, in a sarcastic way, and she talks tough. But she's a sucker for anybody in trouble or hurt.

Most of the guys here, even the pit bulls, are a little scared of her. She won't back down from anybody. People here tell stories about her—how she knocked a guy cold with a sock full of sand, how one troublemaker woke up tied to his bed with duct tape over his mouth. She says these are fairy tales, but most people believe them. Including me.

I sit at Shannon's table for most meals. Sometimes we play poker or Scrabble in the rec room after dinner. She talks a lot, but she's interesting. Except when she's bagging on herself for being fat and ugly—which she does way too much. I hate that. And it's not true. She isn't ugly. She's bigger than other people, but so what?

Anyway, that's Shannon. She jokes that she's "Queen of Camp Feelgood," but that's more or less true.

Question 1: My dorm (log exterior) is built like a motel— long central hallway with rooms on each side. Screens on the windows—wired to an alarm system—to keep us from jumping out. Looking past the screen, I see lawns and concrete walks and other log buildings. Trees and shrubs, a few boulders artistically placed. Everything all neat and tidy like in the brochures. (Parents go crazy with their cameras.)

Off in the distance I can see the dark green of pine forests. That's where I'd like to be. (Don't worry. I won't go coyote-chasing tonight.)

My PS question: Where would *you* like to be right now?
—Rob

Sent: Thursday, November 7 8:34PM
From: Sara4348@aol.com
To: Robcruise99@yahoo.com
Subj: Answer to Rob's PS

Believe it or not, the answer is *right where I am,* living in this hundred-and-some-year-old house at Fort Douglas. No lie! Here, finally, I'm starting to have some friends. Do you know how it feels, being in seven different schools in eleven years? (French only in one, German only in another.) Always saying "goodbye, goodbye, goodbye" to people and knowing you'll never see them again? I've never lived anywhere long enough to have a hometown. (*Hometown!* Now *there's* poetry.)

With the move to Salt Lake, I wanted things to be different. I hoped we could stay. I love the outdoor life here—the hiking and skiing. And I love this school; it's not all military kids. I love the idea of going to the junior prom, trying out for the senior class play, writing for the high school paper. And then GRADUATING! All with the same kids. So that's my answer.

Sent: Friday, November 8 4:05PM
From: Robcruise99@yahoo.com
To: Sara4348@aol.com
Subj: Friday

You surprised me. I figured you'd go for a Paris cafe or a beach on Hawaii. And you picked Utah. I kind of understand how you feel about wanting to be part of a place, going to the junior prom, etc. But it's a whole different world from mine. Different universe, maybe.

Your world: senior class play, dates and proms, school paper. *My world:* Today a delivery truck was parked outside the kitchen. While the driver was inside, Greg (a homefry) crawled under the truck and put his head right behind the back tires.

The driver was already behind the wheel and was shifting into reverse when somebody noticed and yelled. Greg's words to the guy who saved him? "Why didn't you keep your **** mouth shut?"

Sent: Friday, November 8 8:17PM
From: Sara4348@aol.com
To: Robcruise99@yahoo.com
Subj: Friday night

Your take on my world? Wrrrrrrrrrong! It's not the prom dress or a job on the school paper. It's about wanting to have roots. Basically, it's about making connections with people I like and feeling "at home" (whatever that means) where I live. Don't ask me to explain why, but I've found that here. I'm not all pink fluff and ego, Robcruise. So stop categorizing me!

"My world"—to use that shorthand—has for all my life been unpacking and adjusting. I once read a book entitled *Home Is Where Your Feet Are Standing,* but . . . you know what? I've been there, done all that foot shuffling. I'm sick of so much "transitioning." I love being back in the United States and I want to stay put on this quiet little post for a while.
—Sara

Sent: Saturday, November 9 4:05PM
From: Robcruise99@yahoo.com
To: Sara4348@aol.com
Subj: I'm innocent (well, sort of)

Pink fluff and ego—did I say that? NO. Did I ever think it? NO WAY. Did I say that what's normal at your school and what's normal at mine are about a million miles apart? No, but that's what I was trying to say.

And I'm accused of categorizing you. NOT GUILTY. Unless there's a category for people who are talented poets, and skinhead car thieves, and friends to coyote chasers, and who'd rather live in Utah than Paris. (If you know anybody else who belongs in that category, give her my e-mail address. I'd like to hear from her.) Pink fluff? You? You've got to be kidding.

Sent: Saturday, November 9 5:48PM
From: Sara4348@aol.com
To: Robcruise99@yahoo.com
Subj: Reply to Robcruise, Innocence Personified

Well . . . I'm glad we got that cleared up. But please take note: The tears running down my cheeks are *not* crybaby tears. There's a line that guys feed girls, but let me try it on you: I love it when you're mad!

Okay, riled-up friend. After a two-minute deliberation, I pronounce you NOT GUILTY . . . by reason of excess sanity and more-or-less good intentions.

—Sara, Jury of One

Sent: Sunday, November 10 4:05PM
From: Robcruise99@yahoo.com
To: Sara4348@aol.com
Subj: News from an innocent (glad you agree) alien

Hi, Sara—

Breaking news from MU (My Universe): three-for-one trade this week. Remember Greg? (Was it a real suicide try or a fake to get out of here?) He was taken away, and we got three new residents—a girl with purple hair, a guy from Saudi Arabia, and a quiet kid that somebody heard was an arsonist. Right away Shannon brought Masoud (the Saudi) to the aliens' table. Keeping him away from the skinheads.

New physical ed. teacher. I sent him a memo asking about cross-country running as a new sport. He said he liked the idea. Wouldn't that be great, getting out of here and running through the pines?

PS It's been about six weeks since you shaved your head. What's it been like?

Sent: Sunday, November 10 6:22PM
From: Sara4348@aol.com
To: Robcruise99@yahoo.com
Subj: Your last email

Let's face it. I don't write emails, I write letters. From now on, unless I'm mad or rushed, I'll begin with "Dear Rob." It's more natural for me. Living out of the country so much, I've written a million letters (and now emails) to my cousins. I still handwrite letters to Grandpa, the dear old fogy, who flatly refuses to trade his pen for a keyboard.

I keep thinking about your new girl with the purple hair. I hope you'll be nice to her. (I'm identifying.) Can you believe I dyed my hair lime green summer before last, when we were in Liverpool? I was seeing every shade of pastel on the street, so decided to try it myself. Big mistake! Dad tried to lock me in the officers' quarters storage. Mom wouldn't let him, then went to bed with a sick headache. The next day on the street, Gabe made me walk so far behind him, we couldn't talk. So . . . please! . . . be nice to the girl with the purple hair.

As for your PS—my shaved head. Long story. Sure you have time for this?

I would never suggest that anyone do what we four did in thinking we were helping Angie. In the first place, she was embarrassed by it, a reaction none of us expected. And so were we, as it turned out. For about a month everyone wanted to feel our heads, even teachers, and I began to duck whenever I saw a hand coming at me. Worse, Timothy, my supposed boyfriend, was totally turned off by my new look.

When this one really smart senior (the chess champion) called us "a bunch of glory hogs," I knew what he meant. None of us wanted the Big C, of course, but we'd been eating up all the patting and fussing. Now that I'm closer to Angie than ever, I suspect there's something slightly mocking about taking on the mere appearance of being in chemo. In the end, we may have stolen something from her. All *we* had to do was let our hair grow out.

And, yes, I look more like a fledgling chicken hawk than the hairless Chihuahua I was six weeks ago.

Now, one more question for you. Why do you call yourself an alien?

—Sara

Sent: Tuesday, November 12 4:01PM
From: Robcruise99@yahoo.com
To: Sara4348@aol.com
Subj: Aliens

Hi, Sara—

You know what aliens are. They're the ones from another planet. The ones who don't fit in. Every school has them. But it's kind of special here. Of all the weird ones (and we have some real prizes), we're the weirdest.

Thanks for telling me about the shaved-head business. I'm always surprised when you lay things out the way you do. I'm so used to liars and whiners that I hardly know how to act when somebody is completely honest. What can I say that won't sound stupid? I'm glad you're out there, Sara4348.

Sent: Tuesday, November 12 9:11PM
From: Sara4348@aol.com
To: Robcruise99@yahoo.com
Subj: Of weirdos and aliens

Dear Rob,

It's dawning on me that being an alien in that place is a good thing. You're not druggies or would-bes. Not the emotionally unhinged. You're simply aliens. "Outsiders" who don't fit in. Whoa! So, you must ask, "Where *do* I belong?" Easy answer: on the Net with Sara4348, who has a PhD in Outsider Skills.

Oh, wow, I just glanced up. It's snowing! Fat, fluffy flakes. They fly up on gusts, drift, then fly up again, dancing in the lamplight outside my window. What a beautiful sight!

Aunt Ginny, Mom's older sister, is coming for Thanksgiving. She's recently moved to Kayenta, a desert community near the Arizona border, and I can't wait to hear her talk about it. She can make a phone-book delivery sound like a Broadway opening.

I'm awfully glad you're out there, too, Robcruise99.

Sent: Thursday, November 14 4:02PM
From: Robcruise99@yahoo.com
To: Sara4348@aol.com
Subj: News from an alien

The new kid, the rumored arsonist, knew how to make friends. He sneaked in some LSD and some PCP. I heard he had a hidden compartment in his Bible. So we've been having freak-outs everywhere. Three people taken to hospitals.

Still trying to picture Sara on the streets of Liverpool with lime green hair. Anyway, don't worry about Carmen, the new girl with the purple hair. She has lots of company here. We have Day-Glo orange hair, green, fire-engine red, and a guy with red, white, and blue stripes.

Dr. Feelgood shot down my plan for cross-country running. He called me in and took ten minutes to say, "We don't trust you, coyote chaser." If I "demonstrate maturity" this winter, he'll be happy to consider my proposal in the spring. In the meantime—he gave me a big smile right here—I can run around the grounds if I like.

550 days until I turn 18. Then I could go to Utah and watch the snow fall. (None here yet. Just depressing, drizzly rain.)
—Rob

Sent: Thursday, November 14 9:10PM
From: Sara4348@aol.com
To: Robcruise99@yahoo.com
Subj: Dog days of November

Dear Rob,

I'm so sorry your idea was turned down. But don't give up. Just haul out the "sir"s and "ma'am"s—an excellent way to "demonstrate maturity." Can you hold out like he says and try again?

Wouldn't it be great if you *could* come to sunny Utah, out of that rain and drizzle? We'd have a snowball fight for starters. Then I'd hike you up Red Butte Canyon behind Fort Douglas and we'd look for deer tracks in the snow. I'd make us a hot buttered rum afterward and we'd warm our feet by a fire and talk and talk.

I'd rather stay in the dream, but Dad's taking us to his favorite steakhouse tonight (Fat City!). He's at the door downstairs, hollering for Mom and me to hurry. As usual.

Bye for now.
—Sara

Sent: Friday, November 15 4:01PM
From: Robcruise99@yahoo.com
To: Sara4348@aol.com
Subj: Here it is

Here's the poem I've been promising. I kind of cheated. I wrote most of this as an assignment. Our new resources specialist gives us breaks from our Internet lessons and has us do some writing and drawing. She asked us to imagine ourselves in a new place and then show what it was like. The poem isn't really finished, but I can't figure out what else to do with it. So I'm sending it to you anyway. If you fall over laughing, don't tell me about it.

I'm standing by a BUS STOP sign
on Main Street in a town
I've never seen before.

Behind me is a hardware store,
a CLOSED sign in its window
next to barbecues and lawnmowers.

The sun has set,
and the last traces of orange
are fading from the sky.

I look in one direction,
then the other,
wondering which way
the bus will come.

The street is deserted.
The buildings are dark,

except for neon beer signs
in a grocery store window.

Somewhere, far off,
music is playing,
but all I can hear is
the faint beat of the bass.

I wish I could remember where I'm going,
or how I ended up in this strange place.

Suddenly I wonder if some bus left me here.
Maybe I've arrived at my destination
and somebody will come to get me soon.
Meanwhile a cold wind is blowing,
sending leaves and candy wrappers
skittering across the empty pavement.

I shove my hands deep into my pockets
and listen for the sound of an engine.

—Rob

Sent: Friday, November 15 8:26PM
From: Sara4348@aol.com
To: Robcruise99@yahoo.com
Subj: Your poem

Rob, your poem was so worth the wait! You really should post it. Great images! The BUS STOP sign, the CLOSED sign, the bass beat of far-off music. And what could be more forlorn than beer signs glowing in darkened windows? Your poem makes me want to grab a bus—any bus—and come after you.

If this is how you really feel being in that place, I'll disguise myself as a social worker and come get you out. I could do that now, you know. I got my license yesterday.

So keep listening for an engine.

—Sara

Sent: Saturday, November 16 4:01PM
From: Robcruise99@yahoo.com
To: Sara4348@aol.com
Subj: A note from Forlorn Rob

Hi, Sara—

I'm glad you liked my poem. I was nervous about sending it. But you surprised me by saying I should post it. For Iambicpentup and the piranhas? Why would I do that?

So Sara4348 is about to come to the rescue, roaring up the road to Pine Creek in her mom's Camry? I love the idea, but I don't need rescuing right now. I'm okay. Forlorn, maybe, but okay.

I think it's great that you got your license. You'll soon be cruising Main Street, windows down, CD blasting. (Hair flying? Not yet, I guess.)

—Rob

Today's PS: Where did you go the first time you went driving by yourself?

Sent: Sunday, November 17 5:35PM
From: Sara4348@aol.com
To: Robcruise99@yahoo.com
Subj: Sunday afternoon

Dear Rob,

My first solo drive? You would ask. For the first three days I was too scared to take the car out by myself. Mom finally pushed me out the door. "Go, go! We need milk. And get gas while you're there." How thrilling! A trip to the 7-11 for gas and milk. (Disappointed?)

I keep forgetting to tell you. Gabe sent flowers on my birthday, but they got delivered to our sergeant's house by mistake. I was hoping Gabe could get home for Thanksgiving, but he says no way. He's facing finals. But dear Aunt Ginny will be here, with the pies and her famous Dilly Casserole Bread.

Two PSes: 1) What are your plans for Thanksgiving? 2) What pie do you like best—pumpkin, mince, apple, or other?
—Sara

Sent: Tuesday, November 19 4:01PM
From: Robcruise99@yahoo.com
To: Sara4348@aol.com
Subj: Less-forlorn stuff

New license—first trip. I was hoping for a mad dash to a ski resort or a midnight drive across the desert. But right now the 7-Eleven doesn't sound so bad. Anywhere but here.

Bulletin board news: I told you that Shannon posted her poems as MLee1830. That should have been a clue to somebody. Our new resources specialist figured it out right away. Shannon was posting poems by Emily Dickinson (born in 1830) on the board. She loved watching the piranhas pounce on Emily's work.

We have a nine-day break for Thanksgiving. I'm supposed to go to Burbank and stay with my mother—my first trip away since I got here in June. I think it's going to happen.

To the important stuff: If I get a choice of pies, I'll take a slice of each—except pumpkin. That's the one every institution serves—all the time. It must be easy to make. Or cheap!
—Rob
PS How's Angie doing, anyway?

Sent: Wednesday, November 20 3:47PM
From: Sara4348@aol.com
To: Robcruise99@yahoo.com
Subj: (No subject)
Dear Rob,

Great news about going to see your mom. Wonderful, in fact! I hope things work out.

So Mlee1830 is Shannon passing off Emily Dickinson's poems for the heck of it? That is way beyond cool. I'm embarrassed to have been so clueless. Mom gave me a book of Emily Dickinson when I was ten. "I'm Nobody! Who are you?" was a poem I could identify with that year of my invisibility.

The doctor suggested that Angie drop a class or two. She won't, so I've been helping with homework. She's now on meds that control the nausea better, and she's gaining weight. I'll tell her you asked about her. That always seems to pump up her spirits.

Guess what? Aunt Ginny says she'll let me drive her vintage red MG around the post while she's here. It's a stick shift!
—Sara

Sent: Thursday, November 21 4:04PM
From: Robcruise99@yahoo.com
To: Sara4348@aol.com
Subj: Good news from *Unforlorn* Rob

I'm out of here tomorrow afternoon—a van to the Sacramento airport, then a flight to Burbank.

For weeks, my mother has been sending me letters (she doesn't do computers) asking what I want to eat, which museums I want to visit, etc. Probably has a schedule for the whole nine days. All I want to do is get away from Pine Creek and walk for miles. The beach, the mountains, anywhere.

Have fun with that MG. A neighbor in Malibu had one. It was always in the shop. He swore that MG stood for Mechanic's Goldmine.

And send me a note if you can. I'll try to find a computer. Even if I don't, it'll be easier to come back to this place if I know there's some Sara mail waiting for me.

Sent: Thursday, November 21 8:37PM
From: Sara4348@aol.com
To: Robcruise99@yahoo.com
Subj: Good news is right!

For now, goodbye, dear Unforlorn Rob. Happy Thanksgiving! Of course I'll write. And keep trying for a trip to the mountains.

—Sara

Sent: Monday, November 25 10:38AM
From: Robcruise99@yahoo.com
To: Sara4348@aol.com
Subj: (No subject)

I'm in a coffee place called Caffeine and Computers, sipping my hazelnut latte. Great to come online and find a message from you.

Good news first: I've been walking all over the place—mostly on sidewalks. Not easy to find open country around here. But it's great to be moving along, going anyplace I want.

Otherwise, things aren't too good. Stan, my mother's "fiance," says the right things, but his body language says, "You're pig vomit." And my mom is trying way too hard to make things better. Any little thing—burned toast, a spilled drink, Stan not showing up on time—brings on the tears.

She was sick most of the weekend. All her plans down the drain. I keep telling her I'm happy just to be here—away from Pine Creek and walking my legs off. But she keeps on apologizing.

So, Sara, I just shut up and keep walking. If I get really down, I picture you bombing around in that MG. Makes me laugh every time.

Sent: Thursday, November 28 3:09PM
From: Sara4348@aol.com
To: Robcruise99@yahoo.com
Subj: Thanksgiving Day

Dear Rob,

Caffeine and Computers. I'd love to be there, sipping a latte with you. How nice would that be?

I'm sorry about the way things are going. I was hoping you'd have a great Thanksgiving. You know—turkey and mashed potatoes, and football later on. And someone to enjoy it with.

We were all in the kitchen early today. Dad, believe it or not, was doing KP (Kitchen Patrol)—wearing an apron Aunt Ginny thrust at him—and chopping up onions and celery. "Remember that Thanksgiving in Stuttgart?" my mom said out of the blue, and the three of us started laughing so hard.

Overseas the locals don't celebrate Thanksgiving, so we often took in "strays" for dinner—enlistees who were there alone. One cute young private we invited got so sloshed that Dad let him sleep it off on our sofa. He woke up crying the next day. I was only eleven, but I remember that Marcus was from Georgia and called me "a pretty little *thang*." My folks and Gabe thought his accent was totally hilarious, but being called "pretty" was what I liked.

Keep walking. I'll be thinking about you.

—Sara

Sent: Saturday, November 30 1:11PM
From: Sara4348@aol.com
To: Robcruise99@yahoo.com
Subj: Me and the MG

Rob, did you ever get into the mountains? I hope so. But do not (I repeat, NOT) hot-wire your mom's car to get there.

You'll be green when you hear that I got to take Mother Goon out for a spin all by myself. First, so you can picture this, my aunt's car is the genuine old-timey MG roadster, built in 1970.

First, I had to give it a bath and a polish. Like she says, "You want to bond with a car, you have to caress it." (Sneaky way to get a car wash, I say.) Then I got a lesson about what's under "the bonnet." I had to go through the gears a few times—parked. Finally she tossed me the keys and hopped out.

"Write when you find work," she called over her shoulder.

Honestly, sitting in that low-slung driver's seat, I felt like Amazon Woman stuffed into a Matchbox toy. I kept wiping my sweaty hands on my jeans. Finally, I turned the key. The MG bucked a time or two until I got smooth on the clutch, but about the third try I was off. I drove around the Officers' Circle six times. Didn't hit a thing.

In roadster heaven, still . . . Sara

Sent: Saturday, November 30 3:58PM
From: Robcruise99@yahoo.com
To: Sara4348@aol.com
Subj: My Thanksgiving—courtesy of Kinko's!

Hey, this is great! Two long Sara messages. I needed both and got to read them online for once.

I'm sitting at a computer at Kinko's, two blocks from the movie theater where I'm supposed to be. Twenty cents a minute. Thank goodness for the ten-dollar bill I had hidden in my shoe. I'm not "demonstrating maturity," I guess, but the movie was boring. And I felt like talking to you.

My vacation ended early. Everything fell apart on Wednesday. My mother had to be taken back to the clinic. ("Drying out," Stan calls it.) I knew she was close to the edge when I first saw her. She swore she wasn't drinking, but her breath about knocked me over. Anyway, she's safe for now.

I flew back Thursday AM. Had Thanksgiving dinner at the Hometown Buffet in Sacramento. Turkey and mashed potatoes and somebody to enjoy it with—just like you hoped.

Matt, one of the resources specialists, picked me up at the airport. With him were all the guys who had no place to go for the holiday—two skinheads who hate each other, Roland (a drooler), Paul (who talks too loud and smells bad), and Chris (4' 10" with a ten-foot chip on his shoulder). Easy to see why nobody wanted them home.

Matt said that if everybody behaved at the restaurant, he'd take us to a movie on Saturday. So things went pretty well. The only problem was that you can't take food out of the place. Roland loved their chocolate chip cookies. Ate about twenty.

Then he put about twenty more inside his shirt. The manager just waved and said, "Happy Thanksgiving!"

It was snowing when we got back to Pine Creek. I sat up most of the night watching it come down. On Friday we played in the snow like little kids. The skinheads made snow *women*. (Yeah, they were just what you're picturing.) We built a sled run, then had to make our own sleds. Mine was an ironing board inside a garbage bag.

Last night I watched an old Japanese movie called *Rashomon*. Amazing. When it was over, I rewound it and watched it again. By then everybody else was asleep, so I went out and walked in the snow and thought about the movie some more.

In *Rashomon,* the same story is seen through different people's eyes. And each person's "truth" is different. I'm still thinking about that.

I'd better stop jabbering before you fall asleep and before I run out of money. I hope you get another chance to rip around in the MG before your aunt leaves.

Think we'll ever take a walk in the snow together?

—Rob

Sent: Saturday, November 30 4:28PM
From: Robcruise99@yahoo.com
To: Sara4348@aol.com
Subj: (No subject)

Sara—

I'm back at Kinko's. Everything's messed up, and I have to take off. I'll write as soon as I can, but it may be a while. Don't worry. I'll be ok.

—Rob

I started to hit SEND, then stopped. I could almost hear you saying, "Rob, what are you doing?" Then it hit me how stupid this was. I was running away—with no place to go. Almost broke. Freezing weather. And I'm taking off. Dumb. Really dumb.

When I went back to the theater, the van was gone. Woman in the ticket booth said they'd had a big fight. Cops hauled off some guys in handcuffs. She said the cops are still looking for "two boys from some juvie place who ran off."

I was already an official runaway, so I headed out of there. (Figured I had nothing to lose.) But then racing past Kinko's, I decided to send you another note. Glad I did.

I'd better get back to the theater. I don't know what's next. Juvie? Isolation? Whatever, I probably won't be online for a while. Hang on, Sara. You know I'll write as soon as I can.

Sent: Saturday, November 30 5:42PM
From: Sara4348@aol.com
To: Robcruise99@yahoo.com
Subj: (No subject)

Rob, horrible news!

The rumors are true. The post *is* being reactivated and Dad's being transferred. I'm having the most awful meltdown. I can hardly see the screen.

Orders are for Angie's parents to stay here for the next phase (we think because of her treatments), but Dad has to be in London end of December. After a briefing there, he goes to Heidelberg and from there to a base in Turkey or somewhere. I don't know if . . . Whoa, an email. Yours!

I've read it twice now, holding my breath both times. Rob, wow! That was close. Too close! But you decided NOT to run. I'm so glad. You didn't do anything wrong by skipping the movie. Not in my eyes.

No matter what, I'll hang on, I promise. What I don't get is how could everything come crashing down on both of us at the same time? Whatever happened to *fair*?

—Sara

‹DECEMBER›

Sent: Sunday, December 1 4:05PM
From: Robcruise99@yahoo.com
To: Sara4348@aol.com
Subj: (No subject)

Sara, I only have two minutes. I'm sorry, sorry, sorry. I know how happy you've been in Utah. And then—WHAM!—it all gets taken away. What a lousy deal.

I wrote a note today and have it on my disk, so I'll go ahead and send it. Just remember, I didn't know your whole world had been blown apart.

Hi, Sara. Hope I didn't worry you too much with that second panicky e-mail. With the cops after me, I got a little crazy. But I didn't want to leave without telling you. And you talked me out of doing something really stupid. Thanks, Sara. You didn't have to say a word.

After I left Kinko's, I spotted Roland in an alley. He'd run out the side exit when the fight started. (Smarter than I thought.) He was scared, didn't know what to do. I used the rest of my change to buy him an ice cream cone, then had the woman at the theater call the cops.

I told the cops I'd sneaked into a different movie. Said "sir" a lot. They ended up letting Roland and me go back to the school with Matt. The other guys will be in juvenile hall until Monday. Last night the four of us watched *Rashomon,* but I was the only one awake at the end. I had to see Dr. Feelgood today. Got the old Trust and Responsibility lecture. Looked him in the eye and said, "Yessir." (Hard to say that without sounding sarcastic.) I'm now on zero-tolerance probation and the old five-minute Internet, so I'm writing this ahead of time.

Matt called the clinic for me. (Against the rules, but he's a good guy.) They said my mother is "making excellent progress." I hope that's true.

I'm still picturing you tooting around in the MG.

—Rob

Sent: Sunday, December 1 9:11PM
From: Sara4348@aol.com
To: Robcruise99@yahoo.com
Subj: (No subject)
Dear Rob,

I've cried buckets. First with Angie, then by myself. What makes me furious is that our parents knew, *have known,* since the day we all had brunch together. They didn't want to upset Angie, they said, and they didn't think I was "ready."

I'm so sorry I haven't said anything about your Thanksgiving-week email. It was my brightest spot that day, knowing you were having fun and watching that great film. But now, how awful to be back on probation.

No matter what happens, keep me up to date on how your mom's doing, okay? (I'm never sure how you feel about her. Sometimes you seem angry, as if you are talking about a stranger. But I know that isn't the whole picture.)

—Sara

Sent: Tuesday, December 3 4:03PM
From: Robcruise99@yahoo.com
To: Sara4348@aol.com
Subj: Me and my mom
Sara, I know how miserable you are. Wish I could help. Could you live with Angie or one of your friends? What a lousy deal!

You're not sure how I feel about my mother? Welcome to the club. I've been thinking about her. (It's that *Rashomon* movie—how do things look through her eyes?)

I care about her, sure. She's my mother. But she drives me crazy sometimes. When she starts talking about marrying my father, it's soap opera time. Love at first sight, felt alive for the first time, etc.

That's her truth, I guess. But I have a hard time with that whole love-story bit. She was twenty—a junior in college. He was forty-two and married. Everybody (including his second wife) warned her about him—told her how many girlfriends he'd had. But she was sure their love was special. Sure he'd be different now. Duh.

Okay, she was young. I can see her falling for him. What I can't see is why she stayed married to him so long. Even after he was begging for a divorce. She kept pretending everything was fine. ("Daddy's very busy.") She was a secret drinker and took all kinds of pills (but I knew it—I wasn't that dumb). She started having go-go-go highs and stare-at-the-floor lows. (She always tried to hide the lows: "Mommy has the flu.")

Then one day when I was eleven, she signed the divorce papers and signed herself into a hospital. So my father finally got the divorce he wanted, but the joke was on him: He ended up with me. Mom still feels bad about this, says she "abandoned" me.

Memory's funny. When I'm feeling good, I remember the good times. She and I built a whole town out of LEGOs, read *The Wind in the Willows,* waded in the ocean, baked oatmeal cookies. When I'm feeling bad, I remember watching monster movies on TV while she was passed out on her bed. When she was "sick," I fixed food for her that she dumped in the toilet when she thought I wasn't looking.

Does that answer your question? I didn't think so.

Sent: Wednesday, December 4 7:03AM
From: Sara4348@aol.com
To: Robcruise99@yahoo.com
Subj: My life in turmoil

Dear Rob,

Thanks for telling me about your mom. I can understand how you'd have such mixed feelings. Parents can sometimes be *so* unpredictable. Even dense, I'm discovering. Grrrr!

However, things around here aren't as bad as the night my folks dropped the bomb. Like you, I thought of Angie first. I begged until I was blue in the face to be left here, but they'd already hashed that one out and decided it wouldn't work. I'm "too tightly wound" to live with them, Mom insisted, while their family is dealing with Angie's cancer.

What they proposed—as if the idea had just popped into their heads—is that I go live with my widowed aunt Ginny for the rest of the school year. That would be at her place down in southern Utah. (Is that the reason she came for Thanksgiving? To see if she could stand me? Is that the reason I got the MG lesson?) Mom really wants to go back to Germany, hates to be left behind.

"Okay, so let's leave Sara behind," I can hear Dad say (with glee). "Fine with me," Mom would say, just as gleefully. "She's too tightly wound, anyway."

The way we left it, I'm supposed to think it over. Right now, living in a desert community doesn't sound bad. Aunt Ginny works and I'd be on my own a lot. (*That,* more than anything, makes me want to try it.) At least I'd still have my new friend—you—no matter where I was. (Wouldn't I?)

As for Angie, her "numbers" are up again, Mom told me. It's all trial and error, as I see it. (Chemo-of-the-week? . . . Nope, too strong, too noxious. Try another flavor.) Poor Angie! And here I am, a basket case over a simple move. What's wrong with this picture???!!!

Sent: Friday, December 6 4:01PM
From: Robcruise99@yahoo.com
To: Sara4348@aol.com
Subj: Your future

Sara—

It sounds like you've made your choice. A different school, but at least it would be a regular American high school. (I won't mention proms and such. I got in trouble for that. Remember "pink fluff"?)

New schools—I hate the whole thing. We've both had more than our share. I've been trying to count mine. Fifteen anyway. Depends whether I count the ones where I didn't last a whole week (or a whole day). The old Stubborn-and-Stupid Disorder.

I'm sorry you have to do it again. But the desert deal doesn't sound bad. Being on your own and having an MG in the garage—things could be worse.

Demolition derby here. All kinds of drugs. We all get searched, but these people are sneaky. At dinner last night a guy crashed facedown into his chicken soup. Might have drowned if they hadn't hauled him out.

Lousy times. The ones who aren't high are depressed. Roland keeps hanging around me. Guess I shouldn't have bought him that ice cream.

When I think about Angie, I feel like going back and deleting all the stupid stuff I wrote. It all seems so unimportant. But, Sara, I hope things work out for you. I'm rooting for the desert, but they have the Internet in Germany and Turkey. So whatever happens, I'll be around.

Sent: Sunday, December 8 1:37PM
From: Sara4348@aol.com
To: Robcruise99@yahoo.com
Subj: The big decision

Dear Rob,

Another secret revealed: You've been to so many schools, you can't keep track. I can't believe you weren't teacher's pet in all fifteen, smart as you are. But what on earth were you *doing* to drive everyone so nutsy in those schools?

I've decided to live with my aunt Ginny. But you're wrong in thinking her adorable car is a big reason. It isn't, honest. Sitting here thinking about how it all happened, I'm not sure I could explain, but I want to try—maybe so *I'll* understand myself.

I was born into the army, so it's always been my life, the whole culture. I used to be hugely excited by a transfer. We'd haul out the maps, and Mom would get us books and tapes. And I learned more than I ever would have if we'd taken root in Red Dirt, Oklahoma, or somewhere.

But then, along came Fort Douglas and University High. I loved being a regular American kid growing up on American soil—cruising the malls, student hostessing for the Winter Olympics, screaming my head off at football games, skiing with Gabe and his friends. I was "Hard Hat Sara," helping to build a Habitat for Humanity house. Who wants to live on a base in Germany?

Right now, Rob, I'm plenty scared. Mom and I both. We kind of follow each other around the house, being so nicey-nice I can hardly believe it's us. I'll miss my folks A LOT. Incredible as it seems, Mom and I have never been separated.

I just hope I can make it. I'll be holding you to what you said: "Whatever happens, I'll be around." Thanks, dear cyberpal!

—Sara

Sent: Wednesday, December 11 4:56PM
From: Sara4348@aol.com
To: Robcruise99@yahoo.com
Subj: (No subject)

Dear Rob,

Here's some good news and I can't wait to tell you. Angie's folks said she can fly down for a visit once I get settled. Or, if it makes more sense (meaning if she's not well enough), I can come back to Salt Lake for a weekend anytime I please. It's a small thing, but it makes me happier.

You and I forgot all about the PSing. Or at least I did. Oh, well. Living in the fast lane like we are, who needs it? I still have questions, though, and one is: Where are you going for Christmas and when? Back to your mom's?

Here it's a total madhouse. We're all packing like crazy. Angie comes over and tries to help sort my stuff, but we end up sitting on the floor talking. We won't have many more chances. As for Christmas, we've all agreed to simplify. No presents that can't be put in the corner of a suitcase.

What's happening at Camp Feelgood? Things back to normal?

Sent: Friday, December 13 3:58PM
From: Sara4348@aol.com
To: Robcruise99@yahoo.com
Subj: Breaking news

Rob—are you there? Are you still on short rations? Barred from the Internet room? Has something else gone wrong? Two words from you would do it. ("I'm okay," for instance.) You told me to hang on once before and that's what I'm doing.

Things are happening so fast, I have to write again or be totally frustrated. My parents' surprise Xmas gift: We'll be spending nearly a week in NYC before they fly out. I'm so excited about that and everything else, I can't sleep. I can't eat, either, and am down to 118 lbs., skinny for me.

Gabe will meet us in New York for five days. The day my folks leave, I'll fly to SLC by myself, and then (omigod!) I'll drive down to the desert and my new life begins.

Hey, get this! My folks are leaving the Camry with me rather than store it. Can you believe such luck? It's my job next week to see that it gets packed with everything but the fridge.

Coming to you directly from my list (which almost makes a poem):

Books, clothes, boots/poles & skis,
My photo albums and killer CDs,
A destination map from the Internet,
A quilt Grandma made the year she died,
My cell phone and desktop PC,
the 13-inch TV,
and me!

So, for nearly a week, I won't be able to email. I won't know how you are or how you're spending Xmas or ANY-

THING unless you write soon. (Take pity. Could Damian or someone write for you?)

Friday the 13th. I just noticed.

—Sara

Sent: Saturday, December 14 5:50PM
From: Sara4348@aol.com
To: Robcruise99@yahoo.com
Subj: Quick note

Dad has invited me on a "date" tonight, so I'm rushing to get ready. We haven't done this since I was twelve or something. I think he's missing his rebellious daughter already. And I'm missing him. I've wrapped up a book of Stephen Dunn's poems and plan to read him a special one when we get to the Blue Iguana. No word yet from you. How worried should I be? S.

Sent: Sunday, December 15 9:51AM
From: Sara4348@aol.com
To: Robcruise99@yahoo.com
Subj: SOS

Dear Rob,

Now I know for sure. Something is terribly wrong. If I took your silence another way (if you'd decided to end things), this is how it would be, no doubt. But I can't believe that's the case. And I can't believe you'd leave me hanging, either.

Bewildered . . . Sara

Sent: Sunday, December 15 11:09AM
From: Sara4348@aol.com
To: DamianXXXX@yahoo.com
Subj: A request from Sara

Damian, you helped Rob and me out once before, so I know you're a friend of his at Pine Creek Academy. Rob hasn't emailed me for nearly two weeks. I'm worried that something awful has happened. Could you just send a couple of lines telling me when you last saw him and how he is?

Gratefully yours, then and now,

Sara4348@aol.com

Returned mail: Service unavailable
From: MAILER-DAEMON@aol.com
To: Sara4348@aol.com
Sent from the Internet (Details)

The original message was received Sunday, Dec. 15, 11:09AM

*******ATTENTION*******

Your e-mail is being returned to you because there was a problem with its delivery. The address which was undeliverable is listed in the section labeled: "—Transcript of Session Follows—" AOL Postmaster

The following addresses had permanent fatal errors—DamianXXXX@yahoo.com

Sent: Sunday, December 15 3:41PM
From: Sara4348@aol.com
To: Mlee1830@yahoo.com
Subj: A question

Hi, Shannon—

I hope you get this message. Rob Cruise told me about you and your Emily Dickinson ruse, so I'm trying your Mlee1830 with Yahoo!, knowing that's the email service Rob uses.

I'm sorry to bother you, but I really do need a favor. Rob and I have been emailing for quite a while. I've enjoyed his humor and his descriptions of "Camp Feelgood," but he has suddenly disappeared. Now I'm worried. If something has happened to him, could you write back and let me know?

By the way, I've been on the P&W bulletin board, too. They trashed my stuff even worse than they trashed your Emily Dickinson poems. Is that a good sign?

Thanks for your help, Shannon.

Sara4348@aol.com

Sent: Tuesday, December 17 4:01PM
From: Robcruise99@yahoo.com
To: Sara4348@aol.com
Subj: I'm back—FINALLY

Sara, after all that time, it was great to come online and see five messages from you. I knew you'd be plenty worried, but I couldn't help it. (See the message below.) But, Sara, you've got to believe this: No matter what I decided to do, I'd never leave you hanging. I'll read your e-mails tonight and get back to you.

Sara—

I'm getting this ready so that I can send it as soon as we're reconnected with the outside world. The computer system has been down forever. Somebody hacked into the main computer and posted the residents' files for everybody to see—all the staff evaluations, all the confidential comments. They also put in booby traps to foul up anybody trying to repair the system.

I guess one of the residents got busy over Thanksgiving. Or maybe (this is Shannon's idea) one of the residents paid a computer geek to do it. She figures there are more people here with the money than with the computer savvy.

It's been hard going for so long without hearing from you. Are you still headed for Aunt Ginny's? How many times have you changed your mind? And, as usual, I've been wondering about Angie. It can't be easy talking to her. The cancer has to be in the backs of your minds all the time.

Here, besides the computer problems, the big thing is the Christmas break. I'm supposed to go to my dad's place in Malibu, but he hasn't sent my ticket.

He'd better not bail on me. The school will be closed for maintenance and painting, so nobody can stay here. There's talk about a field trip somewhere—maybe Mexico—for the ones who can't go home. Wouldn't that be a great Christmas— going to Mexico with guys like Roland and Chris?

I hope we get back online before then. It's lonesome out here. And with that wild imagination of yours, you're probably picturing me chained in a dungeon or lying on some frozen trail, my throat ripped out by a savage coyote.

Sent: Wednesday, December 18 4:32PM
From: Sara4348@aol.com
To: Robcruise99@yahoo.com
Subj: Rejoice, rejoice!

Dear Rob,

I let out a shriek when I saw *Robcruise99* on my "new mail" screen. I'd nearly given up. Yesterday I was so discouraged I didn't even turn on the dumb computer. Now here you are with a great new email, and I have to leave in thirty minutes. (School choir is singing on Temple Square.) I should wait until after to write, but I can't stand to, so my fingers will fly.

Confession: Robcruise99 online has become *my* secret addiction. Will I have to go to E-Addicts Anonymous? "Drying out" was painful. But I was glad to know that the blackout had nothing to do with you. Or me! I was beginning to lose faith—*bad, bad Sara!*

Yes, I'm still on track for Aunt Ginny's. It's my mom I worry about most, that she'll be lonely w/o me around. That may be egomania BIG-TIME. She'll probably have so much fun playing bridge with the garrison wives that "Sara Who?" will end up being my overseas name this time.

Mom's out warming up the car for me, so I'd better get a move on. Thanks for ending our dry spell. Now I can go back to my normal worries—war, terrorism, the warming earth, on and on.

Suddenly in the mood for carols,
—Sara

Sent: Wednesday, December 18 4:05PM
From: Robcruise99@yahoo.com
To: Sara4348@aol.com
Subj: Your messages

Sara, I came online and got another message from you. It's like Christmas already. I'm addicted, too. It's going to be rough over the holidays. Another e-mail blackout? I hope not.

Here's what I wrote earlier:

Hi Sara—

Good to be back in touch, even for a few days. Printed all your messages and read them over and over.

So you're heading for your new life driving a Camry, with your own cell phone and computer. Way to go! I know it's hard leaving your family and friends, but I'm jealous all the same.

Letter from my mom today. Sounded better. Says she's working on being tougher and smarter. I hope so. But I hoped so last time, too.

Question: "What on earth were you doing to drive everyone so nutsy in those schools?" Answer: Nothing really bad. I just left when I couldn't stand being there any longer. (Sometimes that was soon after I got there. Once in less than an hour.) The old S&S Disorder. I don't know why I thought the next place would be any different.

I'm getting worried about Christmas. The plan was to go to my father's place in Malibu. I'm ready for some beach walking—and maybe a few hikes up into coyote country. But I don't have a ticket yet and haven't heard from him since the computer mess. (I've e-mailed him twice and left a message with his answering service.) He'd better not bail.

Sent: Thursday, December 19 4:04PM
From: Robcruise99@yahoo.com
To: Sara4348@aol.com
Subj: (No subject)

Here's the latest: I won't be going to Malibu. My father's out of the country—probably doing a breast enlargement for a European princess. His business manager called Dr. Feelgood today and is sending money. So I'll be joining the field trip.

Merry Christmas, everybody! For the next two weeks I'll be somewhere on the desert with Roland (the drooler), Masoud (the Saudi), smelly Paul, and Chris (the little maniac). Matt, the same resources specialist who stayed here at Thanksgiving, will be in charge. He's Jewish and says Christmas isn't a great time of year for him anyway.

So, Sara, you're headed for New York, and I'm going camping with Matt and the Misfits. I'll e-mail you if I can. Don't worry about me. I'll be okay. And I won't do anything stupid even if I feel like it right now.

Hope you have a great holiday. I'll be thinking about you. And every time we pass a Camry down on the desert, I'll be checking the driver.

Sent: Friday, December 20 7:01AM
From: Sara4348@aol.com
To: Robcruise99@yahoo.com
Subj: The desert, not the beach?!

Dear Rob,

You may not see this in time, but I'm totally shaken by your news. More disappointments! Go ahead and pretend that Camry you see is me coming for a picnic—with fried chicken in the hamper. Pretend *anything*, but don't get in trouble. Just think of all the stuff you'll have to tell me when we're back on-line.

Dad wants the Camry packed by tonight. "Two days early?" I asked "Don't argue, Sara, just do it." OK, but the PC goes in last.

I won't say Merry Christmas because yours may not come close. But remember, Rob, the really significant stuff is what goes on inside our heads. Excitement, beauty, Xmas joy—the good things we all crave. Don't they all exist first *inside*? I can't get it right what I'm trying to say—I'm too rushed—but I know that *you* know what I'm after. (Omigosh, how special is *that*?)

Take care of yourself (and Roland and Mad Chris and Masoud).

Oh, heck! Merry Christmas anyway!—Sara

Sent: Friday, December 20 3:39PM
From: Mlee1830@yahoo.com
To: Sara4348@aol.com
Subj: Your note

I remember your intriguing poem "Mistaking Identity." I printed a copy, intending to post a critique, but I never did.

It's ironic that your message has introduced another question of identity. You see, there is no Rob Cruise at this school.

Since getting your message, I have been trying to identify Rob Cruise's creator. That shouldn't be hard, but it is.

I assume that "Rob" is in my learning group, as those are the only ones who know about my Mlee joke. That's sixteen people, but only four guys.

Right away I ruled out two fourteen-year-old video game freaks. That left me with Neil and Alex, and I can't see either of them as "Rob." Neil, severely crippled, spends his free time playing Dungeons & Dragons. Alex is a very disturbed boy who never makes eye contact. The rumor mill has him suffering from multiple personality disorder.

Once I ruled out all the guys, I had to start over. That's when I came up with a possibility. Lucinda (Luke) has a crew cut and wears no makeup. She's a smart, sweet girl who's had a tough life. I've heard that she sometimes pretends to be a guy on the Internet. I can't say for sure that she's "Rob," but she'd be my first guess.

You probably know what you're doing, but I'm not sure I'd take the chances you're taking by writing to somebody in this place.

I hope my note isn't too disappointing. I considered deleting your message and minding my own business, but you sounded genuinely concerned. I thought you deserved an answer.

Sent: Saturday, December 21 8:47AM
From: Sara4348@aol.com
To: Mlee1830@yahoo.com
Subj: You're joking, right?

It's been six days since I wrote you. In that time I've had several messages from Rob, the first explaining about the computer mess, so I'm no longer worried. But thanks anyway.

Your email puzzled me at first. I thought "Whoa! What's she saying?" Then it made me mad. I'm still not sure what you intended . . . or how I should react. Your suggestion that I've been writing to a girl all this time is ludicrous. I would know, believe me.

No, Shannon, I think you're putting me on. I don't know

why, but I'm not falling for it. Anyone who can invent Mlee1830 may also enjoy other kinds of "jokes."

Just so you know, I don't intend to stop writing to Rob.
—Sara4348

Sent: Tuesday, December 24 2:31PM
From: Robcruise99@yahoo.com
To: Sara4348@aol.com
Subj: Hi from Las Vegas

Merry Christmas, Sara! I'm in an Internet cafe at a Las Vegas mall. One hour for Christmas shopping. I bought cowboy hats for everybody (big sombrero for Masoud), then called my mother. She's okay—just bummed out about not being with me for Christmas.

Got your sorry-for-me message. No need. Chris picked a fight with two sailors our first night, so we've been staying away from crowds ever since. I love it. Sleeping under the stars. Seeing some wild country. And Matt stops every hour or two and lets us go for a run. Best trip I've ever made.

Christmas morning we'll be in Searchlight, Nevada. (I already know one of my presents. Roland just came running in to show me my barf green Las Vegas T-shirt.) So when you're walking on Broadway, think of me out here in the desert in my ugly T-shirt with a big stupid smile on my face. Merry Christmas to Sara4348!
—Coyote Rob

Sent: Wednesday, December 25 6:47AM
From: Sara4348@aol.com
To: Robcruise99@yahoo.com
Subj: Merry Christmas to you, too, yellow eyes!

It's 6:13 AM on Christmas morning. It's snowing and NYC streets are deserted. I've just opened my first present—your email—which makes me the happiest I've been since leaving Salt Lake.

I just slipped out of my room and came down here to the lobby. The desk clerk and a guy cleaning mirrors are the only ones around. A little coyote whine and a smile got me time on the guest computer.

I couldn't sleep. The trouble is, I've been feeling awfully low—really down there. Mom said I could always change my mind, and I almost did yesterday.

I've been wondering about Shannon. What's she like—really? I mean, is she the kind and honest person she seems from your emails? I just want to know, being as curious a cat as you are.

Uh-oh, the clerk's on the phone and I'm getting pointy looks. Have I been missed upstairs?

—Sleep-deprived Sara

Sent: Thursday, December 26 6:37AM
From: Sara4348@aol.com
To: Angelann@tristate.net
Subj: Merry Christmas from the Big Apple!

Angie, so far away, I miss you soooooooo much!

I'm up early to use the guest computer. The night desk clerk, who saw me yesterday, just brought me coffee. Best news: a note from Rob—sent from an Internet cafe in a Vegas mall. Six of them are traveling through desert country in a van. Imagine spending Xmas in Searchlight, NV—armpit of the nation!!!

I still don't know what to think after that email from Shannon. (Remember, *tell no one!*) I can't believe someone is putting me on, unless it's Shannon herself. If he (or she) *is*, that person has to be very slick! Or very sick! But, Angie, the whole thing is making me sick. Rob just has to be WHO I THINK HE IS!

What am I going to do, Angie? Keep freaking out or tell Rob? I can't wait to see you. . . . We'll talk for hours.

I hope you're feeling better and better. Give Muffy a few pats for me. See you soon, mi amiga!

☺ Love ☺ Sara ☺

Sent: Thursday, December 26 3:19PM
From: Robcruise99@yahoo.com
To: Sara4348@aol.com
Subj: Hi from London Bridge

Sorry things have been so rough for you, but I'm not surprised. Too many changes too fast.

We're in Lake Havasu City. The London Bridge looks pretty stupid here on the desert, but we had to see it.

All the restaurants were closed on the 25th, so for dinner we had hot dogs and root beer. A Christmas weenie roast—how's that for a twist?

Next stop is Organ Pipe Cactus National Monument—three million acres of empty land in southern Arizona. (Matt REALLY wants to keep us away from crowds.)

I was surprised you asked about Shannon. What made you think of her? Masoud and I sent her a tacky postcard the other day—a menu from the Roadkill Cafe.

Hey, Sara—get out and do something you can't do in Salt Lake or the new place. Broadway show? Ferry ride? Whatever. Maybe it'll help.

—Rob the Desert Rat

Sent: Sunday, December 29 11:52PM
From: Sara4348@aol.com
To: Robcruise99@yahoo.com
Subj: Arrived safely

Hi, Rob, Desert Rat! I'm at the Salt Lake airport in the Crown Room—on Mom's card. I have to take a cab to Angie's, but rushed in here hoping to find an email from you first.

Just read your note from the London Bridge. Thanks for not letting me down. You're a genius at locating computers, my wily friend. How do you do it?

It's good to be back in Utah. My nose was pressed to the window from the minute I could see lights—Salt Lake City stretching like a river of jewels right up to the lake. Feels like home. But once again, I'm on my way to somewhere else.

I'll write you from Angie's soon. Right now I'm totally beat.

Sent: Monday, December 30 8:02AM
From: Sara4348@aol.com
To: Robcruise99@yahoo.com
Subj: NYC, etc.

Dear Rob,

Angie's still asleep, but her mom's letting me use the computer in Major Meyer's office. I couldn't let you think I was still moping. The visit to New York *did* improve . . . starting with my attitude. (Imagine that!)

So what did we do for six days in the Big Apple? Ice-skated at Rockefeller Center for starters. Totally cool! Saw *Hairspray*—awesome! Day four we had lunch at the Empire State Building.

Mom wasn't feeling well that afternoon, so Dad took Gabe and me to the Twin Towers site by himself. Dad broke down and cried. He had lost a close friend at the Pentagon on 9-11, but all of us ended up in tears. To *be* there, to actually *see* it—oh, Rob!—it was as if all the horror had been stored, was fresh and waiting for our turn at Ground Zero.

The following day, Mom and I shopped while Dad and Gabe went to a hockey game. We ate lunch at a deli and talked for two whole hours. Mom told me about her and Ginny growing up in this tiny Nebraska town where Grandpa was the only doctor. I guess the girls sort of ran wild—stealing apples and switching people's milk orders, stuff like that. One night they tied a bra on the miniature Statue of Liberty in the park. "Never got caught, either," Mom said in a whisper.

"Mom," I kept saying, "I love hearing this stuff. You guys were soooo bad!"

"Don't tell your aunt Ginny," she goes as we left the deli, "but *I* usually came up with the ideas. Virginia Mae was the nervy one. Insisted we follow through on everything."

Mom had never told me any of this. I'd always thought she and Aunt Ginny were perfect little angels. What a surprise! But sitting there together and laughing . . . I loved it! . . . It was like *we* were the sisters, you know?

The last night in NYC was *supposed* to be our time—Gabe's and mine—to be together, but our time ended up being fifteen minutes in the hotel lobby. Once Gabe's friend arrived, they went off to 52nd and Jazz without me.

My family's gone now. I'm on my own. If I screw up, I

have no one to blame but me. You've been there. You *are* there now. I hope you're not just a spin-off of my wild imagination, someone I made up. I hope you're for real!

Want to make a New Year's resolution together? Do we dare?

—Sara

Sent: Tuesday, December 31 3:40PM
From: Robcruise99@yahoo.com
To: Sara4348@aol.com
Subj: Happy New Year!

Happy New Year, Sara! We're in Yuma, Arizona, and I only have two minutes. Tonight we'll camp out in the desert, away from everybody, but tomorrow we're going to the San Diego Zoo. Got your two messages. (I'd put in a smiley face, but you'd laugh.)

Right now, with day 365 winding down, I just wanted to say that you're the best thing that happened to me this year. I have to go—Rob

PS I'm "for real"—I think.

Sent: Tuesday, December 31 9:12PM
From: Sara4348@aol.com
To: Robcruise99@yahoo.com
Subj: Happy and Wonderful *Wonderful* New Year!

Tomorrow is a BEGINNING! For you, too, dear Rob. I'll be on my way right after pancakes. 300 miles and three summits to cross. Skies are clear tonight, so I-15 should be dry. It's cold as a witch's you-know-what, but I'm ready. I'd never laugh at a smiley face from you—same look I've been wearing since September. I'm glad we discovered each other, too. Miss me! Sara

⟨JANUARY⟩

Sent: Wednesday, January 1 11:04AM
From: Robcruise99@yahoo.com
To: Sara4348@aol.com
Subj: Happy New Year again

Happy New Year, Sara. Great start to the year—a message from you. Okay, here goes— :) (I'll bet you laughed.)

Right now you're driving across Utah by yourself. Sounds like paradise after traveling with this bunch. The gang is at the zoo, and I'm at an Internet cafe, drinking a mocha frappe—starting the year with a little class. Thanks, Matt.

Loved Organ Pipe Cactus National Monument. Miles and miles of open space, incredible plants, birds, javelinas, coyotes, clear skies, and no people. Late at night I'd wander away from our campsite and enjoy the quiet. Sometimes it was hard to go back.

We had a good New Year's Eve. Sitting around a big crackling fire in the middle of nowhere. Matt talked about starting fresh. Had us write down some of the bad things that had happened last year. Then we burned the papers. It probably sounds hokey, but I liked the idea of not carrying all that baggage into the new year.

I've been thinking, Sara. I like your line—"Tomorrow is a BEGINNING." But a beginning of what? I wonder what's ahead. Where I'll be a year from now. Do you think we'll meet this year? (Scary thought, no?)

—Rob

Sent: Friday, January 3 4:47PM
From: Robcruise99@yahoo.com
To: Sara4348@aol.com
Subj: Where are you?

Hi, Sara. I was hoping to get a message, but you're probably not hooked up yet. ☹ (A sad face—hard to believe I did that.) My only message was from my father. He hopes I "continue to make progress," blah, blah, blah.

This is our last night on the desert. Long ride back to Camp Feelgood tomorrow. (How's that for a depressing thought?) May not sleep tonight. May just wander around and listen to the coyotes and look at the stars. Hate to waste any of my last hours of freedom.

Why can't we, just once, be on the same desert?

—Rob

Sent: Sunday, January 5 8:07PM
From: Sara4348@aol.com
To: Robcruise99@yahoo.com
Subj: Are we connecting?

Testing, testing! Searching for Robcruise99. This is Sara4348, wearing a ☺

Hey, dude, I'm back on! I have *so* much to tell you, but no chance yet. Thanks for keeping me posted in the meantime. I'm hoping you guys are back safe 'n' sound, if not thrilled about it. Your description of the New Year's Eve fire made me want to be there.

Hitting ice between Cedar City and St. George, I made a New Year's res. (It was that or start praying!) I'm going to be utterly straight with everyone this year. So here goes some straight talk: I want to know what kind of person Shannon is. I may be jealous, I realize, but there's more to it. Something is not right. I don't know what, but I'm uneasy about her.

You said you got a message from your dad. He's at least thinking of you, Rob. Read behind "continue to make progress." Find anything there?

To be on the same desert . . . ah, yes! Second best, we could hook pinkie fingers over the cybermiles and you could join in my New Year's resolution. What do you say?

School tomorrow. Yikes!

—Your True Sara . . . starting her new life one step at a time. (Not e-z for someone with two left feet and a size nine shoe.)

Sent: Monday, January 6 6:12PM
From: Sara4348@aol.com
To: Robcruise99@yahoo.com
Subj: Life among the roadrunners

Dear Rob,

You haven't had a chance to write back, but I can't wait to tell you how much I love this place. The desert is really something. Already, at 5:03, it's getting dark here. For a few more lucky seconds, I'll be able to see the jagged red cliffs that ring this place—their tips a lovely glowy pink from the sunset. (Look quick, Rob, it won't last.)

Happens every night. Before I ever get my fill of it, the sunlight angles off and the color bleeds away. A dull gray takes over. In another twenty minutes it will be pitch-black outside. You'd need a flashlight.

The week w/o a connection was definitely like stumbling through the desert w/o a flashlight.

All day I've thought about what I'd tell you tonight. I'm limiting myself to the drive down. (Aunt Ginny is having a

Reiki session—whatever that is—so I have the house to myself and a hot chai tea beside me.) But where to start?

I did okay with the Camry. Traffic was light on I-15 and I was cruising. When I stopped at Cedar City to gas up, this guy said ice had been reported on the summit. I was so high about everything right then, I didn't even ask where the summit was. I should have. Twenty minutes into those mountains, doing the limit, I hit ice and lost control.

It was like I was floating. The car was totally in charge and *I was floating*. I got scared, touched the brake, went spinning like a top, and ended up in the median.

Okay, Rob, so this is "just like a girl," but I started to cry. I put my head down on the steering wheel and bawled (to be totally straight). I wasn't hurt and knew I could get back on the freeway, but I was shaking all over. When I looked up, two guys in black leather were coming down the slight embankment toward me. I was so glad to see someone—anyone! The shorter one knocked on the passenger side, motioning that I should roll down the window. (My mother will never hear this story!)

So the guy shoved my thermos and cap off the seat and got in. "We figured you might not be used to driving on ice," he said. So we sat there, with the other guy outside lighting up, and I got a lesson on spinouts. In the end, he offered to take me over the summit, with his buddy following in their SAAB. "You don't have to be afraid," he kept saying. "We'd rather help you than see you brought down in an ambulance."

When he got out to come around to the driver's seat, I could see BIKERS FOR JESUS on the backs of their jackets. For the next 20 miles I heard all about his Harley and his friend's Harley and the trip they'd be taking to Mexico. I've never really believed in angels, but I may start.

If we thought we could meet this year, I'd go for that as my #1 goal. (Yeah, even if it's scary.) To meet may be a little like my spinout, but I lived through that.

—Sara

Sent: Tuesday, January 7 4:03PM
From: Robcruise99@yahoo.com
To: Sara4348@aol.com
Subj: FINALLY!

Hi, True Sara. Just came online and got your message. No computers yesterday—a day for testing and "personal growth" programs. Great to hear from you. I'm glad you're okay after that spinout. Scary—that whole scene. I like the idea of hooking pinkie fingers—over the cybermiles or any other way—but I don't know about that resolution. Utterly straight? With everyone? What about Dr. Feelgood? I'll try to be straight with you, but I think that's my limit. Can you live with that?

I'm surprised that you asked about Shannon again. I got a big stupid smile on my face when I read "I may be jealous." (How's that for being straight?) But you don't have to be jealous of her or anybody else. Time's up. Here's what I wrote Sunday.

True (up to a point) Rob

It's Sunday morning at Pine Creek. Quiet. We got back late last night. A real change to sleep in a bed—with nobody snoring in my ear. Great trip. Even with some cold weather and a little rain. Even with Chris along—whining, arguing, moaning about his rotten parents. He'd get the other guys going, especially Smelly Paul. (Matt says there's some of Chris in all of us. If that's true, it's scary.)

Matt turned out to be a good guy. Knew when to let things go and when to pull the plug. His best idea was stopping every hour or two and letting us run. The first time, I was the only runner. Then Masoud joined me. Then all the rest came along. They moaned, but they liked it.

Masoud was a good sport. Everything was new to him—even the Burger Kings and the Dairy Queens. Funny to watch him doing chores around camp. I don't think he'd ever washed dishes in his life. He doesn't belong at Pine Creek. Says his father, who has mega oil bucks, was worried about kidnappers, and Dr. Feelgood sold him on a prep school in the mountains.

I loved walking on the desert, especially at night or just before sunrise. And I loved lying in my sleeping bag and looking up at the stars. And I loved locating a computer and getting a message from you. It's great being out there alone in that open country, but it's even better when you know there's somebody somewhere who's thinking about you.

Sara, I know these notes go on and on. I hope they're not too boring. I don't talk a lot with other people, but with you—once I get started, I obviously have trouble stopping.

How are things in your new home? I'm ready for a report.
—Rob

Sent: Tuesday, January 7 6:58PM
From: Sara4348@aol.com
To: Robcruise99@yahoo.com
Subj: Mostly about Shannon

Dear Rob,

We're back in sync, more or less. Cool! Thanks for the great details. I love picturing you wandering all night on the desert. But please know that you're never *ever* boring. I want to know all about you, your one-time family, and what's going on with your buddies there. It's *you* who will want to say "Whoa!" to *me*. (Maybe starting now.)

Straight talk here: I have a problem with your sketchy answers about Shannon. So far, what you say isn't making me feel better. Okay, so you're pals, but what else? How did she get to PCA? How does she treat other kids there? Is she what one would call "normal" or stable? Do you believe what she says? Trust me. I wouldn't be asking if I didn't have a reason.

A report on Aunt Ginny and the new home will be coming soon.

—Sara

Sent: Wednesday, January 8 4:04PM
From: Robcruise99@yahoo.com
To: Sara4348@aol.com
Subj: Re: Mostly about Shannon

I'm missing something here. What's the deal with Shannon? You asked me to trust you, so I'll go ahead. But something doesn't feel right.

Shannon's been here at PCA for two years. Came in for substance abuse. Still meets with an SA counselor.

This is the story she tells: She grows up in Southern Cal— big home on the beach. Her mom's a famous model. But

107

Shannon doesn't look like Mom. She's a chunky little kid, and she keeps getting bigger. Mom puts her on diets, takes her to specialists, gives her pills, hires a trainer. But Shannon just gets bigger. She says, "There I was—this fat, ugly kid surrounded by beautiful people."

She started early on vodka and pills. Been in all kinds of clinics and programs. Says she doesn't have a problem now (but she still uses pills sometimes). Says, "I'm really here so my parents won't have to look at me."

She calls herself Queen of Camp Feelgood. Kind of a mother hen for all the——OUT OF TIME.


```
Sent: Thursday, January 9 4:04PM
From: Robcruise99@yahoo.com
To: Sara4348@aol.com
Subj: (No subject)
```
Sara—

Today this little note was on the blackboard in our class-room: WHY NOT TELL 4348 THE TRUTH? I just about fell over. Everybody was asking what it meant. I tried to act dumb, but it was all I could do to keep from screaming.

What's going on, Sara? First you start asking all these questions about Shannon. Then this.

Either somebody's hacking into my e-mail or something's going on behind my back. Which is it?

—Rob

Sent: Thursday, January 9 8:33PM
From: Sara4348@aol.com
To: Robcruise99@yahoo.com
Subj: (No subject)

Dear Rob,

When you had the computer blackout before Xmas, I got really worried. I was afraid something had happened to you. So I wrote DamianXXXX, the guy who sent the birthday message. That came back—undeliverable. I couldn't think what else to do, so I wrote Shannon and asked her if Rob Cruise was all right. (I know what you'll say to all this: "Too much imagination, Sara.")

On December 20 I had a bizarre reply from Shannon. She said there was no Rob Cruise at your school. She said she couldn't even think of anyone who might be writing to me using that name. Her best guess was someone named Lucinda, a sweet girl in your group (who wears a crew cut, she said).

I should have told you, but I was on my way to New York at the time, and besides, the whole thing freaked me out. It seemed like somebody's sick joke. I know that Shannon is your friend, so I couldn't understand why she would write something like that.

Could you just reassure me that you are ROB (my Rob, the one I know) and that you have been telling 4348 the truth all along?

—Sara

Sent: Sunday, January 12 4:04PM
From: Robcruise99@yahoo.com
To: Sara4348@aol.com
Subj: Hi from Lucinda

Sara—

I tried to write you a phony letter from Lucinda. Best line: "In my heart I'm Rob Cruise, and I'm reaching out for you." But I didn't get very far. I was making myself sick.

Come on, Sara. You didn't believe for a minute that I was some pathetic girl, did you? (Yes, there is a Lucinda/Luke here, and she's a real mess, but—do I need to say this?—she ain't me.)

Let me get this straight. You get worried and write to Shannon, and she comes back with this crazy letter saying that Rob Cruise is a girl, and you decide not to tell me about it. Why not? I'm having real trouble with that one, Sara. No matter how I put things together, I come up with the same answer: You didn't really trust me.

Right now I'm exhausted. I can't think of anything cute to add.

—Rob

Sent: Sunday, January 12 5:52PM
From: Sara4348@aol.com
To: Robcruise99@yahoo.com
Subj: My answer

Too bad you didn't finish the Lucinda letter. Sounds like good bedtime reading.

Rob! You must know deep down that I trust you. Otherwise, why would I continue to write as I do? It's the mutual trust (and may I add attraction?) that keeps us online together. We have believed in each other from the beginning.

I'm sorry if this Shannon business has caused you to doubt me. Let's try changing places for a minute. Would you risk our friendship by asking *me* if I was some guy disguising myself as a girl—because Shannon (or someone) suggested I was? I don't think so. How would you ask me, for instance? "Sara, babe, you having some gender confusion I don't know about?"

So what'd I do wrong? I got worried about you when I didn't hear anything. Then along came Shannon's crazy letter. I answered her immediately, accusing her of putting me on.

I know you and Shannon are friends. That's why I can't understand what she's up to. But I'm not thrilled about the idea that she may be having a big old time jerking me around.
—Sara

Sent: Monday, January 13 3:38PM
From: Mlee1830@yahoo.com
To: Sara4348@aol.com
Subj: (No subject)

I know you didn't want to hear from me again. I wouldn't write if it wasn't important.

First, I was totally wrong about Rob Cruise. Worse than that, I didn't take the situation seriously. I was sure that "Rob" was Lucinda's fantasy creation, and I thought you were naive in rejecting that possibility. Being the egotist that I am, I decided to prove you wrong with a juvenile trick. I put a 4348 message on the blackboard and waited for Lucinda's response.

I discovered that I was the naive one. I had completely misread the situation. Lucinda didn't react, but Alex did. I knew then that he was Rob Cruise. I had ruled him out as even a possibility, which shows how limited my view is and how badly I can misjudge people.

First, let me say this: Alex is alive and he's recovering.

Last night he made a suicide attempt. Lying on his bed, he used a knife to sever an artery in his arm. By sheer luck a supervisor came by and saw blood spattered on the window. For the moment, Alex is in the clinic here, and the administration is calling it an "accident."

That's all I know at this point. I don't know exactly what led to this crisis, but I know that my silliness started the whole thing. I am truly sorry for what I did.

The administration here is very secretive about cases like this, but if I learn anything more, I'll let you know.

—Shannon

```
Sent: Tuesday, January 14 3:05AM
From: Sara4348@aol.com
To: Angelann@tristate.net
Subj: Last night's call
```

I'm sorry I kept you up talking so long. I'd rather be on the phone than emailing now, but look at the time. Your mother would kill me.

I haven't slept a wink. I'm so worried about Rob, but I keep thinking about what you said. How do I know that Shannon's "in her right mind"? Is she telling the truth? Rob would be mad if he knew I'd gotten another email from her and not mentioned it, so what should I do? Out-and-out ask him? "Hey, Rob, how much blood did you lose before they found you?" There isn't any way for me to find out *anything*.

A suicide attempt doesn't sound like Rob. Just doesn't fit, but I guess anything is possible. Oh, Angie, I like him so much! This is torture!

Thanks for listening to me go on. What would I do without you?

Much love . . . your best friend, Sara

Sent: Friday, January 17 2:28PM
From: Rolandjacobs123@yahoo.com
To: Sara4348@aol.com
Subj: Hi

Your freind is ok. He will write soon.

Sent: Saturday, January 18 3:50PM
From: Sara4348@aol.com
To: Robcruise99@yahoo.com
Subj: Hellooooooooo out there!

Dear Rob,

Thanks to you and Roland . . . I'm having a better day. This week has been one for the books, hasn't it? I hope you're all right and I hope Shannon has settled down and decided not to bug us.

On the home front here, it's been lonely. I don't have anyone to hang out with yet, so Ginny is finding stuff for me to do—like clean the fridge and fold laundry and bake cookies. (Good grief! I'll be domestic before my time.) But it's okay. We get along just great, and she loves whatever I do in the kitchen. In case you're curious, my caramel-raisin tarts could win the Pillsbury Bake-Off.

Take care of yourself, hear? I'm ready for some news from you. Like where are you and what's happening that Roland had to be your stand-in?

—Sara

```
Sent: Monday, January 20  4:04PM
From: Robcruise99@yahoo.com
To: Sara4348@aol.com
Subj: I'm back
```

Hi, Sara—

Seems like forever since I've talked to you. Hope you weren't too worried. I've been in Isolation for a week—no computer, not even my laptop. Details tomorrow. I really missed you. I've downloaded your messages—☺ (I'll bet you laughed.) Can't wait to read them. I missed you, Sara. I know—I already said that.

—Rob

```
Sent: Tuesday, January 21  4:04PM
From: Robcruise99@yahoo.com
To: Sara4348@aol.com
Subj: Isolation
```

Hi, Sara—

It feels great to be sitting here talking to you. So frustrating last week—all these things I wanted to say to you, and I was totally cut off.

Great having your notes to read. Even the one where you're mad. Tell me about your new life when you get time. And don't hold back on the good stuff—jagged cliffs, fantastic sunsets, driving your car on the desert. Right now you have to have good times for both of us.

Okay, confession time: I did something stupid—again. I was mad on Sunday when I wrote to you, and things got worse. About midnight I couldn't stand it anymore, and I slipped out of the dorm. I walked all over the hills and came back at daylight.

It was the same old story, Sara. I knew better, but I did it anyway. Only this time I got caught.

114

Dr. Feelgood gave me two choices—leaving PCA or spending a week in the Isolation Room. I picked Isolation and even said thank you. Little bedroom and bathroom, just like my dorm room. Except that I didn't see anybody but a counselor (half-hour session every day) and the staff people who brought my meals. No lock on the door. I could leave anytime. But if I left, I was out of PCA. The idea, I guess, is to learn self-control. And how hard it is to live without other people.

On Thursday night they let Roland bring my dinner tray. The counselor said he'd been worried about me. Old pesty Roland—I can't even tell you how good it was to see him. I gave him your address, and he promised to send a note.

Tough week, but I stayed in there. Now I'm under strict probation—five-minute Internet, daily written reports, no un-supervised activities, etc. No complaints, though. Beats Isolation by a mile.

Straight talk, Sara: I was really stupid about the Shannon thing. You wondered what was going on. Well—duh—why wouldn't you wonder?

In the future, if you want to know something, just ask. I'll be as straight as I can.

One thing right now: When I came here to PCA, I felt like Robinson Crusoe—the guy who was all alone on the island. When I had to pick an e-mail name, I shortened that to Robcruise. That name was already taken, so I added numbers. I have other names, but I like Rob Cruise the best.

My Internet time (all five minutes) is coming up. More soon.

—Rob

Sent: Tuesday, January 21 6:33PM
From: Sara4348@aol.com
To: Robcruise99@yahoo.com
Subj: (No subject)

Dear Rob,

Terrible! A whole week of isolation? How'd you stand it? I was feeling cut off and miserable, too, until Roland's note, but real isolation—wow! Now I feel totally selfish, talking about me and my stuff—the glowy pink cliffs, etc., etc., etc. Barf! "Separate Universe" all over again.

Just hang on, Rob! Don't get too far down. I know I'm saying these words from my pleasant little perch, but I mean every syllable. Life is going to look up for you one of these days. Your dad can't keep you there forever, can he? I've never understood what determines when you can leave. In fact, speaking so directly you may never write me again, why do you have to stay there another 482 days? (Remember, you invited me to ask questions.) Have you actually been sentenced by law, by a judge? You haven't told me enough for me to really understand why you have to continue putting up with all that [unladylike word here].

Someday when you feel like it, tell me about your father— Dr. Frankenstein, as you call him. Some terrible things must have happened between you and him.

I'm very happy that you're out of Isolation. I missed you, too.

—Sara

Sent: Thursday, January 23 4:02PM
From: Robcruise99@yahoo.com
To: Sara4348@aol.com
Subj: Lousy Thursday

Hi, Sara. I'm almost ready to go back to the Isolation Room. (I said "almost.") Our resources specialist got a regular teaching job, and she's been replaced by Ms. "Call me Barb" Fortner, who is driving me up the wall. She's big on "group dynamics" and "lowering the barriers to communication." Don't worry, Sara. I'm cooperating—and smiling. It hurts my face, but I'm smiling.

All kinds of fights this week. Maybe because the rain is keeping everybody cooped up. More girls fighting this time. But we're equal opportunity people here. The girls get pepper spray just like the guys.

I probably sound like Chris the whiner, but hey, I'm being straight. (You may decide you want me to lie a little.)

What's happening out there on the desert? Give me all the details. I need some good things to think about.

—Rob

Answer for Straight Sara: I thought I'd told you most of this. When I was in court for stealing the BMW, the judge looked at my rotten record and decided to send me to the California Youth Authority—prison for juveniles. My father's lawyer talked him into sending me to PCA instead. So, by order of the court, I'm here until I'm 18. If I run away or get kicked out, I go back to court. But it's only 480 more days, right?

Sent: Thursday, January 23 8:57PM
From: Sara4348@aol.com
To: Robcruise99@yahoo.com
Subj: 480 more?

Dear Rob,

I'll be crossing off the days with you. Then maybe we'll get to meet somewhere, suppose?

Right now Aunt Ginny is off doing her Reiki thing again, so I can talk to you as long as I please. She doesn't know about you yet, but I'm not far from telling her. She's very savvy, I guess you could say, and already acts like she trusts me.

Okay, since you asked for it . . . what's happening with me?

I finally heard from Gabe and had another email from my folks. Gabe's was all about a ski weekend at Breckenridge, with never any mention of our family's fun in New York. (He's become a college bore.)

Okay, so now I'll attempt to describe Ginny's "habitat." (She's after me to drop the "aunt" part.)

We live on nearly an acre of desert in an adobe-style house that is pinkish red—like all the others here. It has two bedrooms/two baths at opposite ends. A third bedroom Aunt Ginny uses as a home office (she's a dental hygienist in St. George). The living and dining rooms feature floor-to-ceiling views of the red cliffs. My room is on the east. I love that it gets the first bright knock-'em-dead sunlight every day.

There's a built-in desk, where I am now, a purple glider chair where I sit to study, a bed, a dresser, and a Navajo rug on the floor. The best part: I have tall French doors leading off my room and out onto the patio. I slip out there every night and practically freeze to death staring at the stars.

So far I've seen two comical roadrunners (or the same one twice), lizards, Halloween-size spiders, families of quail, and rabbits, both the soft bunny variety and the big rangy jacks. We hear coyotes yipping at night, but I haven't seen one yet. During full moon, they run the gullies and howl.

Enough. Almost. When I asked Ginny about rules (Mom said I had to), she burst out laughing. "We'll make them up as we go along," she said. "If you get too far out of line, I'll strap you down over an anthill." When I laughed, she added, "Don't think I won't!"

We had fun shopping last Saturday. I got some platform shoes and a long black skirt. We ended up with big bowls of chili at the Bear Paw, where Ginny told me about her first crush. This kid had braces, the old-fashioned kind with slimy rubber bands. He lisped, so she took up lisping herself to keep him company. What a nutcase! Suppose that's why she became a hygienist?

School stuff later. This is too long already.

—Sara

Sent: Monday, January 27 4:03PM
From: Robcruise99@yahoo.com
To: Sara4348@aol.com
Subj: More Internet troubles

Hi, Sara. I don't know if you'll get this tomorrow or next year. The computer system is shut down. Hackers again. (Why couldn't they do this when I was in Isolation?) On Friday morning the PCA home page had a picture of Dr. Feelgood's head pasted on a sumo wrestler's naked body (all equipment in plain sight).

For the last three days, I've been trying to write about my father and me. It's hard. I start writing, then get mad and quit. But here it is—my version, anyway.

My father is a famous plastic surgeon. Gets special treatment from hospitals and other doctors. And he's rich enough to get special treatment in most other places. He's used to getting what he wants—and fast.

He wasn't around much when I was a baby. My mother raised me. With her help, I learned to read early. All of a sudden, I was reading cereal cartons and billboards. Then, for the first time, my father got interested in me.

I remember him smiling while I read to him from his medical books. I didn't understand any of it, but I could get the words out. He got a kick out of using me at parties. They'd hand me a book, and everybody would get quiet while I read. Then they'd all clap and say what a smart kid I was. I loved it.

Dad was sure I was a genius. Sent me to special schools. Paid big money for tutors. Figured I'd graduate from Harvard at fifteen or something. His son—the Wonder Boy.

For a few years, things were fine. Good teachers and lots of attention—how could I go wrong? But then the trouble started. Some subjects, especially math, weren't so easy for me. He figured I must have a bad teacher or I must not be trying hard enough. So, pretty soon I'd be at a new school with new teachers. And I'd be getting these lectures about making use of my "gifts."

Too bad, Dad. I was good at some things, not so good at others. He got more and more disgusted. (So did I. And I knew how to fight back—forgetting my homework, failing tests on purpose.) Instead of Wonder Boy, he had Super Brat on his hands.

When I went to live with him, things got worse. He decided I was spoiled, needed discipline. So he sent me to military schools and prep schools. (Got me out of the way—a big plus.)

I didn't stay very long at any of them. I didn't fight or cause trouble. I just left when I couldn't stand it any longer—slipped away and headed for open country. (And sometimes I stole a car to help me get there.) I'd camp in the hills until somebody found me. Then it was juvenile hall, a hearing, and a trip back to Malibu. And the whole thing would start again.

Fast forward to the BMW and Camp Feelgood. I guess it all sounds pretty stupid. (It does to me, and I was there.) I can just hear you saying, "What was the matter with you? Couldn't you see how you were messing up your life?" Good questions. But this is the part that's hard to explain: Sometimes you can get so down and so tired that you just don't care.

—Rob

Sent: Monday, January 27 8:34PM
From: Sara4348@aol.com
To: Robcruise99@yahoo.com
Subj: (No subject)

Dear Rob,

Thank you for telling me. It couldn't have been easy, laying out personal details. I'm honored that you decided to trust me. I admit that I cried reading it. Painful stuff! With layers and layers of disappointment, your dad's as well as your own.

With what I know now, I can understand why you're there. But Camp Feelgood is only for *now* until you have proved you're NOT what your police record would have the world believe.

As for all that agony growing up, isn't it possible to . . . I don't know . . . shuck off all the bad stuff? Get rid of it? Leave it in a steaming heap somewhere behind you? Things are different now. I know you're not rotten (far from it) and you know it, too. I also know you're trying to make the best of a really bad situation.

You may end up my hero if you keep on like this.

—Sara

PS Where shall we meet in 476 days? Can we wait that long?

Sent: Wednesday, January 29 4:02PM
From: Robcruise99@yahoo.com
To: Sara4348@aol.com
Subj: 474 days to go

Let's meet in Searchlight, Nevada. After living in this zoo, I'll be ready for somewhere really quiet.

Your talk about dumping the past ("leave it in a steaming heap"—I love the way you put things) made me think about our New Year's bonfire. Remember that? We wrote down the bad things from last year and burned them. Matt says, "You don't have to be a prisoner to your past." I like that idea. And I believe it—most of the time.

New thought: When we were in Las Vegas, Matt drove us along the Strip past all the big hotels. One of them has a roller coaster on top of the roof. Maybe we should meet there. Start out a little crazy.

Don't worry about me. I'm okay. I've learned to smile while I grind my teeth—very helpful with our ding-a-ling resources specialist. And the rain is slacking off. I may get to run around the parking lot tomorrow.

Best of all, I have a friend named Sara4348 who says I may end up her hero. (I almost put in a smiley face, but that didn't seem very heroic.)

See you on the roller coaster.

—Rob

Sent: Thursday, January 30 5:38PM
From: Sara4348@aol.com
To: Robcruise99@yahoo.com
Subj: 473

Dear Rob,

A roller coaster in Vegas? Good choice! My Camry could have me there in two hours. (Actually, I was thinking of something more exotic—like Victoria Falls in Africa. Guess I'd better get that job I keep talking about.) But, hey, let's keep working on this. We have plenty of time.

It's too bad we can't be here talking face to face, burrowing our toes into the soft sand of the big gully. Knowing me, I'd want to hold your hand, too. Not because I feel sorry for you. (Please don't think that.) But because we are talking about what honestly matters to us.

I wish I had more time. My aunt has asked her girlfriend and her daughter (who goes to Dixie High School in town) to make a run with us to Mesquite on the Nevada border. Ginny wants to show me the Joshua Tree Forest—acres and acres of these funny old-man cactuses—and would like me to make friends with McKenzi.

It makes me feel better knowing you're out running, even if it is just in the parking lot. (Good grief, the parking lot!)

—Sara, who would settle for Searchlight in a pinch

Sent: Friday, January 31 4:01PM
From: Robcruise99@yahoo.com
To: Sara4348@aol.com
Subj: Friday

What a picture—you and me holding hands and digging our toes into the sand. I need a little fantasy right now, and that's as good as it gets. (Victoria Falls isn't bad either.)

I saw Joshua trees on our trip. Funny old-man cactuses—great description. (I'm glad you don't say *cacti* either.)

I'm having trouble with the new resources specialist. Even with all my fake smiles. Today she wrote me up as uncooperative because I didn't want to read my essay to the group.

Weirdness here. Shannon's on something. Says she isn't, but I know the signs. At dinner last night she started joking about why Masoud and I were avoiding her. Did she have bad breath? Were we allergic to smart girls? Then, all of a sudden, she was crying her eyes out. Everybody likes old Shannon, so in no time other people were crying along with her. Finally she looked up and told Roland to quit bawling. He tried, but she poured ice water down his back anyway. So the whole table ended up laughing.

How about Seattle? Take a ferry to one of the islands?
—Rob
PS When do I get to hear about your school?

‹FEBRUARY›

Sent: Sunday, February 2 1:35PM
From: Sara4348@aol.com
To: Robcruise99@yahoo.com
Subj: Cliffside School for the Performing Arts

Dear Rob,

Tell you what. If you keep on COOPERATING, I'll write ahead and reserve tickets for two on the ferry. Deal?

Okay . . . so, here it is: *SARA'S TAKE ON THE NEW SCHOOL.*

To start with, it shouldn't have surprised me that kids who go to a performing arts school are (duh!) *performers*. But I never dreamed they'd be performing nonstop, that they'd be so "on" all the time. Believe me, it's the first thing you notice here. Everyone lives at center stage, regardless of looks or talent.

Sometimes it feels like you're in the middle of one big audition. Walking down the hall, you hear voice warm-ups, someone wailing on a sax, piano music—Schumann to Gershwin. Even conversation is oh-so-dramatic. Seems that no one ever relaxes into being "just a student."

So what am I doing at a place like this? Beats me! I don't dance, sing pop, play an instrument, or act. But Aunt Ginny found a loophole—my writing. A patient of hers who teaches at Cliffside mentioned that they were desperate for yearbook staff (the school being only three years old). They needed someone who could organize, crack the whip, and write the schlock. Enter Sara.

In some ways, it's exciting. I love it that classes are small and that schoolwork is easy. In warmer weather, I hear, classes move outside. Can't wait for *that,* since the school's setting is a huge natural amphitheater (see brochure). It's true. We're surrounded by towering Navajo Sandstone cliffs. No sports other than fencing and riding.

School lets out at 2:30. Early release works for rehearsals and kids who have jobs. I signed up for study hall alternating with yearbook last period of the day. That's where I got to know Joel, my only friend to date.

The school is kept small—150 to 200 students. It's a treat, I admit, coming from a school of 1800, to feel like I might have a voice in things. If only everyone wasn't so posey and dramatic!

I hope you won't mind if I forward parts of this Cliffside stuff to Angie. I can't go through writing it all again. She's doing better, by the way, and says she'll be finished with her last batch of chemo well before Easter. (She also wrote that she *thinks* she has a boyfriend. I'm not sure what that means.)

If you haven't fallen asleep reading about my new school and you haven't jeopardized our *one-and-only connection,* write and tell me what's happening with that resources specialist. I also need continuing updates on Shannon, Masoud, Crazy Chris, and the girl with the purple hair.

—Sara

Sent: Monday, February 3 4:04PM
From: Robcruise99@yahoo.com
To: Sara4348@aol.com
Subj: Updates

Sara—Reading about your school, I had a great idea. An exchange program. We send you a drooler, a homefry, and a skinhead; you send us a sax player and an actor. (No, make that a dancer. We have too many actors here already.)

Cliffside sounds pretty good, even with the always-onstage types. (We have them here, too.) The red cliffs, classes outdoors, and school over at 2:30—I'd trade you any day.

In fact, right now I might trade with somebody in juvenile hall. Just to get away from "Call me Barb." Yes, Sara, I'm cooperating—fake smiles, the whole bit. But it's tough, especially when she tells me to let my heart speak.

Updates: Crazy Chris has shaved his head and joined a skinhead group called the Demons. Masoud is learning lots of English. The girls think he's cute, and they're always helping him. Carmen (purple hair) dyed her hair jet-black and is now carrying a Bible. Shannon's up and down. The aliens kind of tiptoe around her, never knowing what to expect.

And me? I'm sitting here with a stupid smile on my face, thinking about the Seattle ferry.

—Rob (Mr. Cooperation)

Sent: Tuesday, February 4 8:10PM
From: Sara4348@aol.com
To: Robcruise99@yahoo.com
Subj: More updating

Dear Mr. Cooperation,

The exchange proposal left me howling. And you're right, as usual. I do have a pretty ideal school situation here. I wish you had half as much freedom. I end up with hours and hours to think about ferry rides and all that good stuff. I am lucky.

But I haven't been so lucky in making friends. Have I mentioned Joel, who has yearbook/journalism with me? My list starts and stops with him. We began sitting together on the bus (mornings only) when it was obvious we were the "Lone Rangers." Mostly we bitch about school, but he also talks about his job at the pancake house—the IHOP. (Little does he know that job-hungry Sara is taking mental notes on everything he says.)

Joel lives on a small ranch out in the country, so is the first one on the bus every morning. His specialty is mime. I've only seen him perform in whiteface once, but he's very good. He said he'd teach me the basics, but I don't know when he'd find time. Weekends he works either at the IHOP or hauling cattle feed for his dad. (Can you imagine a stranger combination—the ranch kid doing mime?)

I like the two girls I met at Xetava, the coffee shop out here, but they're totally wrapped up in each other. McKenzi calls me a lot, but isn't someone I relate to. Her big thing (finger down throat) is makeup. Mention lip gloss or mascara and you get a shopping channel testimonial.

I've been thinking more about Shannon, about her weird behavior. How could someone so smart and funny end up so . . . kind of twisted? Have you figured it out? Maybe she's just "letting her heart speak." Like teacher says she's supposed to.

Okay, so how about this kind of trade? I'll send you a marimba player and you come and write yearbook copy with me. After school, we could walk all over this desert looking for coyote tracks and desert tortoise trails. (I love it that you like to walk so much. Did I ever tell you that? Walking is the best way I know to get important thinking done. I've been doing a lot of it lately.)

Say, has anyone ever walked between Pine Creek Academy and southern Utah for the pure heck of it? We could be the first.

—Sara

Sent: Wednesday, February 5 3:38PM
From: Mlee1830@yahoo.com
To: Sara4348@aol.com
Subj: FYI

I don't know if Alex/Rob has written to you, but I know you must be concerned about him. He is doing very well. The wound on his arm has almost healed, and with his new medication, he seems more relaxed than before.

He has rejoined our learning group and is making an effort to work with our new resources specialist. This is a challenge, as her teaching approach, emphasizing discussion and spontaneous writing, is not suited to his personality.

I think they can learn to work together. Although she finds him difficult, she recognizes his ability. She was very impressed with his latest piece, a horror story about a girl submerged in a car. She thinks he should try to publish it.

By now, Alex may have told you most of this. I hope so. Either way, since I was the one who gave you the bad news, I wanted to share the good news with you.

—Shannon Walker

Sent: Thursday, February 6 4:02PM
From: Robcruise99@yahoo.com
To: Sara4348@aol.com
Subj: Thursday

Hi, Sara. Straight talk, okay? That's what we promised for the new year. I don't know how to say this without sounding like a jerk, but here goes. I'm glad you found a friend, somebody to sit with on the bus, etc. I just wish your friend's name was Josephine or JoAnn, not Joel. (Yeah, I'm jealous. Can't help it.)

Tough times right now. "Call me Barb" is always on my

case. The good news is that she thinks I am "a talented young man" with "incredible potential." (Are you impressed?) The bad news is that she thinks I need to set myself free—whatever that means. And she's trying to help me do it by making me talk. ("How do you feel about that?" "All of your friends would love to hear what you wrote.") Sometimes I want to scream, "LEAVE ME ALONE!" But I don't. I just pull back the corners of my mouth and grind my teeth. Tah-dah—Mr. Cooperation.

Walk to southern Utah? Hey, that'd be one way to set myself free. (Probably not what Barb has in mind.)

Sent: Friday, February 7 5:38PM
From: Sara4348@aol.com
To: Robcruise99@yahoo.com
Subj: TGIF!
Dear Rob,

This "straight talk" is amazing, isn't it? Your one little ol' word, *jealous,* left me grinning big. If I knew how to be coy, I might make the most of what you're admitting. But the truth? I'm mostly interested in Joel's job. He probably wonders why I ply him with questions all the time and why I showed up for breakfast last Saturday at the IHOP. Not to worry. Joel has studly good looks, but we're just buds. It's cool, though, that we can talk like old friends.

Last night after school I missed the bus and had to walk the five-some miles home. I was really bummed until I spotted an endangered desert tortoise crossing *under the road,* using one of the little tunnels built for their protection. I may be one in a million who actually *looked for and witnessed* turtle traffic.

Have to rush. Ginny and I are going to dinner and a movie. Soon as she gets home.

I wish you hadn't lost your old teacher, Rob. What a pain! But this "Barb" must be pretty smart if she recognizes your talent. So keep on cooperating. Even if it kills you.

—Sara

Sent: Sunday, February 9 4:04PM
From: Robcruise99@yahoo.com
To: Sara4348@aol.com
Subj: Waiting

Hi, Sara. Lousy times right now. I don't know what's coming. Here's the story.

This time I got in trouble almost by accident. (I know—that sounds like Chris the whiner talking.) On Friday our learning group was doing fast-writing exercises—ten minutes without stopping. The writing was supposed to be private, but Ms. F kept wanting people (mostly me) to volunteer to read theirs aloud. I just fake-smiled and said mine was too personal.

Then she told us to write about the color blue. I muttered, "I can't think of anything to write." Right away Shannon banged down her pen and said, "I can't either." Then everybody else banged down their pens. "Pick up your pens!" Ms. F shouted. We did. "Start writing!" Most of us just sat there. She wrote us up for "outright defiance" and named me as the ringleader.

Dr. Feelgood is in New York right now, so we have to wait until Tuesday for our punishment. I don't know what to expect. I may be finished here. So I'd better tell you Happy Valentine's Day now. Happy St. Patrick's Day, too.

But you have to believe this, Sara. I'll be back as soon as I can. I don't know when, but I'll be back.

—Rob

Sent: Sunday, February 9 8:40PM
From: Sara4348@aol.com
To: Robcruise99@yahoo.com
Subj: Not again!

Rob, I feel terrible. Right now, Emails R Us. Talking back and forth . . . it's all we have.

Okay, so a few days without won't hurt us, but maybe your writing group's "rebellion" will. My sage advice? See *Rashomon* again and give the new teacher another chance. I know, things must have seemed insufferable to you, but teachers are allowed to have peculiarities, too. Maybe she's never had a class like yours. Maybe she's intimidated big-time. Maybe she's as scared of you kids as you are sick of her.

If you can't make it past Ms. Fortner's little experiments, how will you get through another year and onto that Seattle ferry? Come on, Rob!

A promise to go on: a kinder, gentler email in a few days when I've calmed down.

—Sara the Scold

Sent: Monday, February 10 7:04PM
From: Sara4348@aol.com
To: Robcruise99@yahoo.com
Subj: Featuring Sara

Dear Rob,

How many days incommunicado? The verdict comes tomorrow, right? This may be a miserably long week. Remember the game "Pile On" that we used to play as kids? That's how I'm thinking of your plight—with you at the bottom of the heap, unable to breathe.

I'm home alone, rare for a Monday. Ginny is off to a dental hygienists' seminar in Vegas. She'll crack them up with her stories about the OPMs, overprotective moms who won't let their kids come into the examination room alone.

I mainly wanted to tell you about the cool talk Ginny and I had after the movie. She took me to this funky little place for lemon frozen custard (reminds her of her high school hangout—red Naugahyde booths straight out of *American Bandstand*).

After the custard, I got up my nerve and told her I wanted to look for a job. I told her I wanted to earn money—for a car when Mom claims hers and just for the experience. The clincher, I think, was letting her know how serious I was. Her first reaction was to ask if I'd like to work at home for her—doing billing and accounts. I didn't say "No thanks," but she could see it in my face.

There was a long, miserable pause after that, and my heart sank. When she finally looked up, she said if *I* thought I was old enough and reliable enough, it was okay with her. She went on to say that having to cope with new situations had left me with "an impressive maturity." (Her exact words!)

"Your mom may kill me," she added, "but, hey, with two of us working, we can hire a cook."

Now, your turn to tell me everything. I hope Dr. Feelgood will be in a good mood when you see him.

—Lonesome Sara

Sent: Wednesday, February 12 4:04PM
From: Robcruise99@yahoo.com
To: Sara4348@aol.com
Subj: 1 story & 2 answers to 2 notes

Story: Tuesday afternoon. Dead quiet in the room. Ms. Fortner is checking papers and giving me rotten looks. Shannon hands me a note: GET CREATIVE. WRITE HER A BIG SUCK-UP APOLOGY. I almost laugh. Me? Apologize? No way. But then I catch myself. The old Stubborn-and-Stupid Disorder again—and look where it's gotten me so far.

So I spend about an hour writing a little short note and hand it to Ms. F. She reads it and gives me this superior smile. But she's not letting me off that easy. She wants me to crawl a little. She says, "Would you like to read this to the group?" The old S&S Disorder almost kicks in, but I fight it off and read the stupid note. Ms. F lets me read half of it, then says, "Louder," and has me start over. When I finish, Shannon pipes up, "That goes for me, too, but I didn't have the guts to write it." Everybody else says, "Yeah." "Call me Barb" smiles, and we don't even go to Dr. Feelgood's office.

Dear Sara the Scold,

Internet sessions were canceled on Monday, so I got your chewing-out note after this happened. Now aren't you sorry?

To the Sara who wrote the second note—

Looking for a job. Great. (I'm jealous.) Good idea not to work for your aunt. Wouldn't be a real job that way.

Happy Valentine's Day to both of you Saras! Why don't the three of us meet at Ginny's frozen yogurt place?

—Rob

Sent: Friday, February 14 7:08AM
From: Sara4348@aol.com
To: Robcruise99@yahoo.com
Subj: Welcome back!

A box of chocolates couldn't be sweeter: *Rob's back online, and he's not too mad at me.* So Happy Valentine's Day to you, too, and a big bag of smilies.

I'm sorry that Sara the Scold came out while you were "away." She's actually Sara the Scared in disguise. I was so afraid we'd never get to meet if things went on as they were. I knew you were trying—all that stiff smiling. But how awful to be humiliated—made to read your apology aloud. That Fortner is a real sicko! I hope nothing else happens.

I *do* know that life at Camp Feelbad can get really complicated. I also know deep down that you're a good person. So hang with me when I turn snarly and forget what I honestly know.

The '50s place Ginny took me? Perfect! I'll save up my nickels for the jukebox. It lets loose with a cascade of bubbles when you make a selection. Ginny and I played "Sixteen Candles" three times and drove the other people crazy.
—Gotta run to catch the bus. S.

Sent: Friday, February 14 4:05PM
From: Robcruise99@yahoo.com
To: Sara4348@aol.com
Subj: A valentine poem

I wanted to send you a poem for Valentine's Day, but I couldn't get anything finished. So you'll have to settle for a Gabe-type job.

A valentine secret
That I've never told:

I like all the Saras,
Even Sara the Scold.

—Rob

```
Sent: Friday, February 14 6:36PM
From: Sara4348@aol.com
To: Robcruise99@yahoo.com
Subj: My perfect day
```

A poem for ol' Sara the Scold, of all things. She doesn't deserve it. Thank you, thank you, from all of us Saras!

Guess what? I'm interviewing in the morning. The message was on the machine after school. Didn't dream things would move so fast. Right now I'm going through my closet for something—anything!—that will make me look like a good hire prospect. Yes, don't worry, my hair has grown out to a bouncy length and my teeth are gleaming (Ginny's whitening systems).

Hey, I too have a secret. I know about this totally uninhabited Pacific island. Do you like beaches?
—Sara

```
Sent: Saturday, February 15 3:38PM
From: Mlee1830@yahoo.com
To: Sara4348@aol.com
Subj: Alex
```

This is a difficult note to write. I am not a hysterical person, but I am very frightened.

Yesterday our resources specialist, Ms. Fortner, tried to get Alex to participate in our project, a series of collaborative poems. When he wouldn't, she ridiculed him.

When she left the room to use the copy machine, Alex began to swear. This was surprising because he never swears. And he didn't sound right. His voice was higher, and the words came out much faster than usual.

He stood up and headed for the door. He didn't look right. He walked differently, and he looked different. He was bent over, and his eyes were half-closed. And he kept swearing. Then he said, "I'm going to kill her. First I'm going to cut out her tongue. Then I'll cut off that nose." Then he turned toward us and said, "And none of you can stop me."

This is hard to explain. The person talking just wasn't Alex. Everything was different—the words, the voice, the movements.

When he turned back to the door, he banged into a desk. And everything changed. He was Alex again. He straightened up and looked around. He seemed kind of surprised and embarrassed. He walked back and slid into his chair. Later, when I asked if he felt all right, he didn't seem to know what I was talking about.

As you can imagine, the whole group is worried. We've talked to the people in charge, but they think we're exaggerating. So we still have Alex with us. I don't know much about multiple personality disorder. That may not even be what he has. I just know there's something inside Alex that is very frightening.

Obviously, I'm afraid of what might happen next. We are all being very careful. If I were you, I'd do the same. I'd change my e-mail address and try to forget the whole thing.

—Shannon

```
Sent: Saturday, February 15 4:05PM
From: Robcruise99@yahoo.com
To: Sara4348@aol.com
Subj: That island
```

A totally uninhabited island? Let's go. Now.

```
Sent: Saturday, February 15 5:01PM
From: Sara4348@aol.com
To: Angelann@tristate.net
Subj: Freaking out . . . again!
```

Forwarding Shannon's latest. Should I tell Rob? (Oh, help!) Look for a phone call around nine tonight. Love you! S.

```
Sent: Sunday, February 16 8:44AM
From: Sara4348@aol.com
To: Robcruise99@yahoo.com
Subj: (No subject)
```

I'm packing, I'm packing! But I can't go yet, I got the job. You can guess how it came about. Joel told me about an opening. So I rushed over and applied. I must have seemed "impressively mature" during the interview, because I am now a hostess-in-training at the local IHOP. Twenty hours a week. If I do okay, I'll get to be a waitress—my goal. (All those tips, plus good experience for a college job.)

Much to do. I hope working and all the rest won't eat up my Rob time.

—Sara

Sent: Sunday, February 16 4:05PM
From: Robcruise99@yahoo.com
To: Sara4348@aol.com
Subj: Your job

Way to go, Sara! My latest fantasy: showing up for breakfast at IHOP and having Sara bring me a huge stack of pancakes. What are you going to do with all that money?

Weird time here. I could use some advice. I'll try to write about it tonight.

Sent: Tuesday, February 18 4:03PM
From: Robcruise99@yahoo.com
To: Sara4348@aol.com
Subj: Now what?

Sara, I'm in a mess. I feel really stupid about it. I should have seen it coming, I guess. But I didn't. The whole thing was a complete surprise.

Last Tuesday Shannon asked me to help her. Said she needed somebody who could listen without making judgments. I wasn't crazy about the idea. (People on drugs can go on and on and on.) But I owe her. I was really messed up when I first came here—living inside my head, not talking to anybody. She had me sit at her table and made people leave me alone.

So Tuesday night we sat on a bench outside the rec lounge, and she talked about her sad life. In detail. From fourth-grade sleepovers to vacations in Hawaii. Really depressing. The next night things were a little better. She was mellowing out, sounding more like the old Shannon.

But then on Valentine's Day, right in the middle of a story, she stopped, looked over at me, and said, "I love you."

I couldn't believe it. This was old Shannon, my bud. I just sat there with my mouth hanging open. But once she got going, she wouldn't stop. Said she'd loved me from the start. How could I not know it? Couldn't I tell?

No, I couldn't tell. It never crossed my mind. I tried to make a joke out of it: "Come on, Shannon. We're buddies, remember? You can always find a lover. But you'll never find another buddy like me. Don't mess things up."

That didn't help at all. She says, "It's because I'm fat, isn't it?" I say she looks fine, but she's sure I'd like her better if she looked different. And she keeps wanting to talk.

Typical stupid conversation:

Me: I just don't feel that way.

S: Why not?

Me: I just don't.

S: That's no answer.

Now she's all bummed out and high on pills. She keeps giving me these I'm-in-pain looks. I feel sorry for her, but I don't know what else I can do.

That uninhabited island sounds better all the time.

—Rob

Sent: Tuesday, February 18 7:19PM
From: Sara4348@aol.com
To: Robcruise99@yahoo.com
Subj: (No subject)

Before you start feeling sorry for "poor Shannon," Rob, you'd better see the emails she's sent me since Xmas. I'm forwarding them to you now, and you'll instantly know why. My hope is that they'll give you a more complete picture of Shannon and will help answer some questions.

She's got to be hurting, I agree with that. And I'm sorry for any part I've had in making things worse. But I don't know what to do. I've deliberately not answered her emails. But if you're really Alex and there's "something inside" you that is all that scary, now's the time to let me know.

Obviously, I haven't changed my address. Just as obviously, I'm not about to delete yours from my list.

—Sara

Sent: Thursday, February 20 4:04PM
From: Robcruise99@yahoo.com
To: Sara4348@aol.com
Subj: A question of identity

Dear Sara:

Let me introduce myself. My name is James Martin. You have become a source of conflict in the lives of Shannon Walker and Rob Cruise. As is usual in these cases, it is my duty to intervene.

In an attempt to sever your connection with Rob Cruise, Shannon Walker approached the truth. She suggested that Rob Cruise was one of several personalities housed within a single mind. She failed to disclose the full truth: that she herself is another personality housed in that same mind. In short, Rob Cruise and Shannon Walker are two identities sharing a single body. Your involvement in these persons' lives creates grave difficulties for me, as well as others. You see, Sara, I too share that body.

Nah! Come on, Sara. You didn't believe any of that, did you? Or maybe you did. If you can swallow that suicide story, who knows what you might believe? Hey, I read the notes. I know that Shannon is a really good liar—all those sneaky little details. But multiple personalities, and me severing an artery? Sara, Sara, you're smarter than that.

I dumped the notes in front of Shannon. She just smiled. "I did it for you," she says. "I wanted to scare her off. It's the best thing that could happen to you. You've been running away all your life. You'll never get straight unless you start facing reality. The last thing in the world you need is some dippy fantasy girl you've never even seen."

So that's Shannon. She's not a bit sorry, and she acts like I did something wrong. The worst of it is that I'm still in the learning group with her—all day, every day. I'll make you a deal, Sara. Instead of a big apology, send me some good news. I need something good to think about right now.

—Not-That-Weird Rob

Sent: Saturday, February 22 9:22AM
From: Sara4348@aol.com
To: Robcruise99@yahoo.com
Subj: A reply to my esteemed e-person

Dear Mr. Cruise:

The next time you begin a correspondence with a fledgling poet, be more forthcoming. Right at the outset, say, "One of my personalities would like to email you." Or, maybe, "All of the persons housed in this body like your poem. Write us back."

Okay, as you request, I'll spare you another apology. But I'm ready to duke it out with you over the remark: "You're smarter than that." *Huh*-uh! Being cautious (and sometimes frightened) in today's world *is* being smart. Do you realize that if we girls don't have built-in predator detectors by the time we're ten, we're lost?

Now, are you ready for the really frightening truth? You (and yours) are the one(s) being stalked. Shannon is the well-meaning person who tried to halt the stalking. Haven't you wondered why I've tried to lure you out of the country . . . off the continent . . . to a remote island?

Ginny is yelling "Are you about ready?" from the other room. We're going shopping so I won't look like "a poster girl for the needy," to quote my crazy aunt. I mean, I *am* a working woman now. Guess I need to look a bit more fetching.

More soon, if I haven't been too serious a disappointment to you and James Martin, etc., etc., etc.

—Sara

Sent: Sunday, February 23 4:03PM
From: Robcruise99@yahoo.com
To: Sara4348@aol.com
Subj: Stalking

Sara—

You have my permission to stalk me anytime.

Ugly times here. Shannon is getting weirder by the day. I'm staying as far away as I can, but it isn't far enough.

—Rob

Sent: Monday, February 24 4:10PM
From: Sara4348@aol.com
To: Robcruise99@yahoo.com
Subj: Speaking of Shannon . . .

Dear Rob,

I still feel bad about Shannon. I can see how she could be in love with you (no problem there), but for you to have someone that interested in you and not know it . . .

Truth is, I don't have much experience in this area, although I've probably been what you call "in love" about 29 times. (No, 30, come to think of it.) Mostly, you end up getting hurt. My guess is that girls get hurt more than guys because they're *always* in love. (Girls love guys and guys love cars.)

My best advice? Watch your back. Shannon's feeling mortified and may decide to show it.

—Sara

Sent: Tuesday, February 25 4:04PM
From: Robcruise99@yahoo.com
To: Sara4348@aol.com
Subj: (No subject)

Don't worry. I'm watching my back, my front, and everything in between.

You still owe me good news. Tell me about your job, your school, your aunt, anything—except the thirty times you've been in love. (I'm not ready for that right now. In fact—straight talk—I may never be ready for that.)

—Rob

Sent: Wednesday, February 26 7:19PM
From: Sara4348@aol.com
To: Robcruise99@yahoo.com
Subj: (No subject)

Rob, I've never *ever* been in love. Not really. Only crushes. (Didn't 30 sound like a few too many?) All I can say is how sorry I am for this whole messy situation. I know you'd like to disappear every time you see Shannon. *But remember, you didn't do anything wrong*. You were probably sort of dumb, not picking up on how she felt, but you were only trying to help.

Whatever happens . . . DON'T CRAWL OVER THE FENCE AND RUN! I'll never get to see Searchlight if you do.

—Sara

‹MARCH›

Sent: Sunday, March 2 4:51PM
From: Sara4348@aol.com
To: Robcruise99@yahoo.com
Subj: Are you still there?

Dear Rob,

Best news: Cliffside is organizing a climbing club and will be getting an instructor for three days, a cool climber from Salt Lake. He's coauthor of *Wasatch Climbing North*. Actual climbing will only be two hours a day after school, but Snow Canyon is so close we can be on-site in five minutes. I can't wait.

Worst news: *no news from you*.

But here I am with a whole hour tagged "Rob." I'm taking an e-z out to update you on Sara-happenings. A list. So just print it out and bear with me.

1) I had an email from Heidelberg. My folks are fine. Mom sounds secretly pleased that I have a job, but she can't say so. I think she still sees me as about twelve.

2) Gabe wrote about staying at Angie's to ski on Presidents' weekend. That's what Gabe and *I* should have been doing. Looks like I'm out of the loop these days when it comes to my brother.

3) Next week I'll be trying out for *Anything Goes,* the spring production. (How am I going to fit everything in?)

4) Joel is riding with me to work and back. His mom is ecstatic that she won't have to pick him up past midnight on weekends anymore. I'm ecstatic because he's buying gas.

5) Other job news? Learning everything is lots harder than I expected. I like the nice people who come in to eat. Okay, so kids rattle me a bit when three of them want to sit at three different tables and the mom has no opinion.

More about me and you'll be wishing you were in Ushuaia—my latest idea for a meeting place. It's at the southernmost tip of South America, jumping-off spot for Antarctica. Warm and fuzzy doesn't exist down there.

—Same old inquisitive, impatient Sara

Sent: Thursday, March 6 4:01PM
From: Robcruise99@yahoo.com
To: Sara4348@aol.com
Subj: I'm back

Sara—

Two notes from you. Yaaaay! No time to read them now. Here's what I wrote last night. I wish I had better news. But, hey, with two new notes, things are already looking up.

Sara—

I hope you're not worrying too much. Same old story. Lost all my privileges for a week. Last Wednesday night outside the dining hall, Chris (remember him?) jumped on my back and started whaling away. A security officer gave us both a shot of pepper spray. Horrible—like being on fire. Shannon told Chris I'd called him a crybaby. She wanted me in trouble—and off the Internet. And her plan worked.

Shannon is still strung out—and getting scarier. Sometimes she just sits and stares at me. She's talked to Ms. Fortner about me. (You know about Shannon's lies.) Now Ms. F treats me like total slime. Asks me snotty questions, hoping I'll talk back. But I smile and COOPERATE like crazy. I can't get in any more trouble.

I might be smart to get out of here while I can. I can pass for eighteen. If I got some little job—farmwork or kitchen work maybe—who'd bother to check my age?

I know how you feel about this, Sara, but things may get so bad I won't have a choice. I know you worry, but I'll be all right. You have to believe that. Here's the deal for now: If you don't hear from me, things are okay. It just means I've lost my privileges again. If I take off, you'll know right away. I'll send you a note from a cyber-cafe.

—Rob

PS Think they need dishwashers in Ushuaia?

Sent: Friday, March 7 7:09AM
From: Sara4348@aol.com
To: Robcruise99@yahoo.com
Subj: (No subject)

NO! NO! NO! You're smarter than that, to quote someone I like very much. You'll be on the run the rest of your life if you don't stick it out now. Please—I'm begging you—listen to me! YOU HAVE TO STAY!

Worked late, am running late. Was feeling sick, but went anyway. Now I'm sick over what you're planning to do. Write immediately and let me know you've changed your mind.

—Sara

Sent: Friday, March 7, 4:02PM
From: Robcruise99@yahoo.com
To: Sara4348@aol.com
Subj: Your notes

Sara—

What a way to start an e-mail—NO! NO! NO! (How do you *really* feel?) I'm trying, Sara. You have to believe that. Here's what I wrote earlier.

Loved your notes, especially the job stuff. I don't know about that rock climbing, though. Never tried it, but it looks scary.

I've been reading your old notes about places to meet. They all sound good—even Ushuaia. (I'm a warm-weather guy, but I'll get some long underwear and earmuffs.)

Things are still bad here. I fake-smile my way through the day. Then in my one free hour I run as hard as I can around and around the parking lot. It helps. And so do notes from Sara4348, who is still welcome to stalk me anytime.

—Rob

Sent: Sunday, March 9 9:48AM
From: Sara4348@aol.com
To: Robcruise99@yahoo.com
Subj: Thanks!

Dear Rob,

Your Friday email was the best medicine yet. I folded up the printout and put it under my pillow so I could read it whenever I wasn't dozing. I've had the flu, slept a lot for two days.

I was so sick during yearbook on Friday that I lost my cookies in the girls' room. (How embarrassing!) Joel got so worried he waited outside the door, yelling in, "You okay in there?" (We'd been taking yearbook pictures when it suddenly hit me.)

Joel called his mom, and she picked me up in their beat-up old truck. What a nice lady. Insisted on coming in and helping me into bed. She gave me a little foot rub, a thing my mother used to do when I was sick. I nearly cried. And then, just hearing her making tea in the kitchen . . . all those familiar sounds . . . obviously, I'm missing Mom.

So, Rob, I'm not this big tough girl I thought I was.

I'm glad you're hanging on. I was so afraid you'd take off. They probably do need dishwashers in Ushuaia, but I don't think you want to be one of them. Especially not in your long johns and earmuffs.

Write/tell all. YES! YES! YES! (Is that better?)

—Sara

Sent: Tuesday, March 11 4:02PM
From: Robcruise99@yahoo.com
To: Sara4348@aol.com
Subj: Some YES! YES! YES! for a change

Hey, Sara, break out the smiley faces— ☺ ☺ ☺ ☺ ☺ . I've been rescued—by Matt, the guy who led our Christmas trip. When he heard about my trouble with Shannon and Ms. F., he got me switched to his new learning group (twelve guys, no girls). The other guys all have learning problems, but I'm there as a peer counselor. (Me a counselor! How's that for a twist?)

The whole thing is fantastic. We eat a half hour earlier than the others, so I hardly even see Shannon. I'll keep getting my lessons from the Internet, but Matt also gave me a list of books I should read. Today I started *Desert Solitaire*. Mainly Matt wants me to help with physical activities. You should have seen me today getting these couch potatoes to run around the soccer field. (They call me "Coach"!)

Last night's dinner topic: Who's tougher, Hulk Hogan or the Destroyer? If Matt's students work hard all day, they get to watch a video at night, and they love old wrestling tapes.

So things are better. Lots better. I'm out of that mess. And I'm reading good books. And I'm learning about hammerlocks and choke holds. What more could a guy want? (Well, a visit from Sara for one thing—but you get the idea.)

—Smiling Rob

Sent: Wednesday, March 12 3:10PM
From: Sara4348@aol.com
To: Robcruise99@yahoo.com
Subj: Run, Robbie, run!

Dear Rob,

It's about time! You finally have a life you can run with. Gimme five! Then enlarge this self-portrait and hang it on your wall.

~:-) Smiling Sara (with hair)

Your news made me so happy I pigged out on a whole pint of pistachio-nut ice cream last night.

"What are you *doing*?" Aunt Ginny screeched when she came in after work and caught me. "I'm celebrating, can't you tell?" I generously offered her the nearly empty carton, but she shoved it back. "What on earth would you be celebrating, you little maggot?"

Then guess what I did. I sat there at the kitchen island and told her about you. We finished a whole pot of green tea between us and skipped dinner entirely. She was totally fascinated and listened almost without interrupting.

"So that's why you're always staring at that monitor," she said when she got up. "I was afraid you'd turned into some kind of computer nerd." We laughed and hugged. She made me listen to the usual "But you have to be careful, Sara, and realize that everyone isn't as *trustworthy* as you are." In the next breath she added, "But I agree. He sounds like a keeper. Just use your head."

I have to stay online tonight and download some boring data for school. Haven't forgotten Ushuaia, but *brrrr!* Now I'm feeling more like a sunny spot in the Bahamas. Heard of Harbor Island?

Hey, Rob, I think there's a bit of Edward Abbey in you. I bet you'll love *Desert Solitaire.*

I ask you . . . who is out-smiling whoooooooooom?

—Sara

Sent: Friday, March 14 3:24PM
From: Robcruise99@yahoo.com
To: Sara4348@aol.com
Subj: Another world

Hi, Sara. Busy week. Yesterday I moved to a new dorm and changed my Internet time. So now I'm with Matt's crew full-time.

This is a new program. Matt thinks these guys will do better away from the others—in a place of their own. Most of them have been picked on and ridiculed all their lives. They have learning problems and all kinds of behavior problems—like a bunch of wild little boys. (Remember Roland, the drooler? He's one of this gang now.)

I still have time for my own work. Matt has a regular aide—Bernice, everybody's grandmother—so I help mostly with recreation. (We run every day—trying to burn off some of that energy.) All the guys are friendly—too friendly sometimes. They want to sit by you, tell you jokes, give you high fives, show you stuff. It can wear you down. But I'm still glad to be here.

Shannon handed me a note today. Says she wants to talk. Just what I need.

Letter from my mother this week. She's living in a halfway

house, working at a restaurant. Said she's not worrying about the future, just wants to be a good employee. Maybe things will work this time.

E-mail from my father. He has moved. He didn't say so, but I think he's getting a divorce.

I finished *Desert Solitaire*. Now I want to go to Arches National Park. Hey, Sara, maybe we could meet under Delicate Arch at sunrise.

Or sunset. Or noon. Anytime.

—Rob

Sent: Sunday, March 16 10:48AM
From: Sara4348@aol.com
To: Robcruise99@yahoo.com
Subj: So much good news . . .

Dear Rob,

You must be turning cartwheels. I love your descriptions of the Wild Bunch, how needy and slap-hands-friendly they are. They're totally lucky to have a "big brother" like you. Now I just hope that Shannon won't jump in to be the big spoiler.

Boy, do you read fast! *Desert Solitaire* is not an easy book and you're already finished. What are you into next?

Delicate Arch at sunrise may be the best idea yet. We could both actually get there, for one thing (the most important thing). And Arches is a place I've never been. Shall we shoot for that? (I hear there's climbing, too.)

I have to tell you what happened. Last night Joel took me to an ides of March party at Casey's house. Mostly Cliffside kids. Punch and pizza inside, people going out to their cars for beer and pot. Casey had a mike set up and we were doing karaoke—"Ain't No Mountain High Enough" and "You're So Vain." Everyone got pretty silly and loose and it was fun.

About midnight the Ecstasy started around. "Five bucks a pop," Casey chirped at me with her hand out. I told her I was too cheap, but what I really wanted right then was to grab Joel and go on home. (Who needs *artificial* ecstasy? Ginny says she has to scrape me off the ceiling most days as it is.)

Right after that a drunk kid threw Casey's cell phone onto the porch roof. "You jerk!" she screamed. "It's my mom's. She'll kill me!"

We were all outside by then, so I got busy casing a drainpipe that ran up the corner of the house. I knew I could shinny up there. And—hey!—nobody else was offering. So . . . wearing a pair of Casey's tennis shoes, Sara comes to the rescue. Piece of cake!

I was up on the roof, doing a crazy little victory dance before tossing down the phone. Suddenly I was hit in the face with a blinding light, and realized that everyone below had quit clapping and hollering.

"Stay right where you are!" came a man's voice. It was the cops. So the party broke up, and I had to sit in the patrol car for a 15-minute lecture before I convinced the officer I wasn't "on" anything, that I was just doing Casey a favor.

Do you think I'm weird, Rob? I love parties, but I don't need any of that stuff. Now my biggest worry is that Aunt Ginny will get wind of my midnight climbing spree.

Say, Rob, that's terrific news about your mom. Nothing wrong with working at a restaurant, bub!

"Sunrise. Or sunset. Or noon. Anytime." (Pure poetry!)
—Sara

Sent: Monday, March 17 3:23PM
From: Robcruise99@yahoo.com
To: Sara4348@aol.com
Subj: Happy Saint Paddy's

Happy Saint Patrick's Day, Sara. Our gang is having a mini-parade tonight—green clothes, stupid hats, shamrock cookies (from Bernice), and Matt playing "My Wild Irish Rose" on a recorder while everybody else bangs on drums (wastebaskets).

Funny weekend. Matt usually leaves on Friday afternoon, comes back Monday morning. His replacement is this crazy ex-marine named Victor—about fifty and tough as nails. Rides his bicycle thirty or forty miles to get here, runs the place like a boot camp. He's big on self-defense, calisthenics, and martial arts videos. But he obviously likes these guys, and they love him.

Okay, serious talk for a minute. Do I think you're weird? I hope you are. And I hope you stay that way. I hate all drugs and booze—you know that. Look at my mother. And Shannon. And all the rest. All these morons who think drugs are cute and cool ought to spend some time with the deadeyes around here, watch them slobber while they try to think of a word.

Okay, I'm done preaching. But that's the way I feel. All the studies say that kids of substance abusers are likely to be abusers themselves. Not me. No way.

I'm supposed to see Shannon tonight or tomorrow. Even with all the stuff she pulled, I feel like I owe her.

I just read over the note about your aunt. I like her. Hey, maybe we could get her together with Victor. Make a great pair.

Delicate Arch at sunrise. Wow!

—Rob (still smiling)

Sent: Thursday, March 20 8:15PM
From: Sara4348@aol.com
To: Robcruise99@yahoo.com
Subj: Ginny and Victor

Dear Rob,

You must be out of your tree. I can't exactly see Ginny as a match for your weekend marine. Maybe a description is in order.

- She's petite (two inches shorter than I am)
- She's brunette (hair longer than mine)
- She can still do the lindy (I never could)
- Her favorite TV is H&G (Gag a maggot!)
- Her books? Dental hygiene, mysteries, and *AOL for Dummies*

What she and Victor *do* have in common? Uniforms! Hers consist of white slacks and shoes, polyester tops in Popsicle colors. She, too, is big on self-defense and says she has a pink belt in karate. (Not so sure I believe that.)

My hostessing job is going great. I just wish people wouldn't be so, well, *human*. "What's in that new chicken fajita salad?" one of my Alzheimer's customers asks—every single time! I go nutsy with dumb questions like, "Is this table going to be right in the sun if I sit here?" (Yup, your sitting there may cause that to happen.) Or last night, from this guy who looks exactly like Mr. Rogers: "Look, sweetie, don't put any little kids near me. I'm seriously allergic."

Picturing your Saint Patrick's parade left me laughing so hard Ginny came in to see if I was choking. Thing is, I am sleep deprived and getting sillier by the minute. (Don't mind me!)

—Sara, working woman experiencing fatigue

Sent: Friday, March 21 3:23PM
From: Robcruise99@yahoo.com
To: Sara4348@aol.com
Subj: Re: Ginny and Victor

I'll write in a day or two. Don't worry. For once I'm not in trouble. Keep smiling at the dumb customers. It's good practice.

—Rob

Sent: Sunday, March 23 3:22PM
From: Robcruise99@yahoo.com
To: Sara4348@aol.com
Subj: Sunday

Sara—

Sorry to be gone so long. I just couldn't stand to write about what happened.

I talked to Shannon Monday night while the gang was watching their wrestling video. I could tell she was wired. She admitted it, said she'd been having a hard time. Then it was the same old stuff: What could she do? What if she lost weight? I said everybody, including me, would like her better if she got off those lousy pills. She said she could quit for me. If I really cared. And pretty soon she got back to her mother and how hard it was growing up in that house. On and on.

Finally I said, "Listen, Shannon, this is just the meth talking, and I'm tired of it. If you really want to talk, lay off the pills for a day. Then we can try again."

She took a swing at me, then spit at me when I jumped out of the way. "Forget it!" she yelled. "Get outta here. I'm sick of looking at you." So I went over to the dorm and watched wrestling.

I guess she went back to her room and swallowed every pill she had. She went out of here in an ambulance. The official

160

word was that she was "seriously ill." Matt told me later: She was in intensive care for two days, is now at some rehab place.

I keep thinking about what I might have said. (At first I tried to make her laugh, which made things worse—like I wasn't taking her seriously.) And I should have had Matt talk to her counselor right away. I just didn't think she'd do something like that.

So Shannon's gone. I liked her—right from the start. Until she got so crazy, she was one of the best friends I ever had. I don't know what else to say, Sara. It's just so damn sad.

Sent: Sunday, March 23 6:04PM
From: Sara4348@aol.com
To: Robcruise99@yahoo.com
Subj: Shannon

Dear, dear Rob—I'm so sorry.

What can I say to make you feel better? Nothing except *that*—how sorry I am for Shannon, and for you, too. Why did she have to do it? She must have been utterly depressed. Now *you* feel guilty because you think you might have changed things. I doubt if you could have, but I can tell how awful this makes you feel.

It *is* damn sad, but, Rob, how lucky that she lived. Now maybe she can get the help she needs somewhere else.

I hope you won't beat yourself up over this. You couldn't have been a better friend to her. Just try to keep that other person in the forefront—Shannon at her best, her funniest, her quirkiest.

(And if it's possible, be a little glad that she loved you, you know? It's not a bad thing.)

I wish I was there to hug you.
—Sara

Sent: Sunday, March 23 11:38PM
From: Sara4348@aol.com
To: Robcruise99@yahoo.com
Subj: Second thoughts

Dear Rob,

Tonight after writing you, it occurred to me that none of this would have happened if I hadn't written Shannon in the first place. I mean . . . it hit me like a slap in the face. Due to my meddling, someone nearly killed herself. It was dark and spitting rain, but I grabbed my coat and tore out of the house.

I must have walked miles. The only company I had was Robert Frost, my first poet. I kept thinking of his "I have been one acquainted with the night." Bleak, but exactly how I felt.

I hope you're in a better place right now and are sound asleep.

Yours . . . Sara

Sent: Monday, March 24 7:02AM
From: Sara4348@aol.com
To: Robcruise99@yahoo.com
Subj: The latest here

I've just had a phone call. Word's out about the climbing clinic—three afternoons this week, with the last two hours each day for real climbing in Snow Canyon. Also, each night at 7:00 we have dance rehearsals for *Anything Goes*. (I begged off to work Wednesday.) I hope you can still email me, but I may get behind temporarily. Just wanted you to know.

How are you feeling?

—Sara

Sent: Wednesday, March 26 3:23PM
From: Robcruise99@yahoo.com
To: Sara4348@aol.com
Subj: About second thoughts

Sara—

Henry, one of the gang, says, "You look sad." I tell him I am a little sad. He looks at me for a second, then says, "You want me to tickle you?" My kind of counselor.

Matt says, "This is about Shannon, not you. Shannon's choices. Not yours." That sounds cold, but I think he's right.

It's easy to get into the blame game. It's my fault because I didn't handle things right. It's your fault for "meddling."

And let's blame Shannon's parents for raising her wrong and then dumping her at Pine Creek. And let's blame Ms. F. and Dr. Feelgood on general principles. And we're just getting started.

Why can't we just feel sad without feeling guilty?

Okay, I confess. I talk a good no-guilt game. I still fall into the coulda-shoulda trap. (I coulda done this and I shoulda done that.) But I'm working on it.

The good news is that Shannon's alive and in a rehab program. In a week or two she'll probably be queen of the place.

Delicate Arch at sunrise. See you there—if you can fit me into your busy schedule.

—Rob

Sent: Thursday, March 27 3:22PM
From: Robcruise99@yahoo.com
To: Sara4348@aol.com
Subj: A pome

Hi, Sara. I thought you might need a little poetry in your life. (Apologies to Gabe.)

Rob says to so-busy Sara,
Who hasn't a minute to spare-uh,
"I know that it's tough,
But one line is enough
To let me know you're still there-uh."

—Rob

Sent: Thursday, March 27 6:37PM
From: Sara4348@aol.com
To: Robcruise99@yahoo.com
Subj: *One-liner:* answer to charming "pome"

Formed by wind and rain erosion
on Entrada Sandstone,
the salmon-colored Delicate Arch,
even at sunrise,
is 45 feet high and 33 feet wide.

Sent: Friday, March 28 3:23PM
From: Robcruise99@yahoo.com
To: Sara4348@aol.com
Subj: Another pome from Rob

I came online with this little jewel and found your Delicate Arch piece. My poem doesn't fit now, but I worked too hard on the dumb thing not to send it. A real e-mail soon—I promise.

There is a young lady named Sara
Who hasn't a second to spar-uh.
If climbing, school, and job

Make her give up poor Rob,
She'll be making a serious erra.

```
Sent: Saturday, March 29 8:10AM
From: Sara4348@aol.com
To: Robcruise99@yahoo.com
Subj: Running, but loving your pomes!
```

How many more *pomes* can you get out of my four-letter name? (What if they'd called me Hortense?) I got home late from rehearsal, but couldn't fall asleep after your email because I was doing a GO/SEARCH on my brain for rhymes. Seems only fitting to return a "pome." But what rhymes with Robcruise? *Top shoes? Sob news?* Or how about the mad preacher who started to *lob pews?* Then I remembered my haiku assignment—about climbing:

First Rappel

Blinded by sun and fear,
airborne, earthbound, the climber
thinks of her mommy.

No erra, I'm your Sara.

```
Sent: Sunday, March 30, 3:22PM
From: Robcruise99@yahoo.com
To: Sara4348@aol.com
Subj: Finally—time to talk
```

Sara—It's Saturday night. Victor has the gang watching a Jackie Chan movie, so I have time to write a note.

I like Victor better all the time. Amazing energy. He

must give a thousand high fives and handshakes over a weekend.

Today we had a dorm cleaning followed by a military-style inspection. Victor told me, "I don't care about having things clean. But these boys need to do something they can be proud of." The gang did a great job, and they *were* proud.

I really liked your "First Rappel." It inspired me to write my first haiku.

Picturing you there
hanging from a cliff, I think,
"You're too smart for that."

We have spring break in a week. I'll probably stay here. My mother is still at the halfway house. She's getting an apartment soon—but too late for my break. And my father is off in Switzerland. I asked Matt about another desert trip, but he's headed for New York to visit his family.

Today I went to the Arches National Park Web site and looked at pictures of Delicate Arch. Great pictures, but two things wrong—it wasn't sunrise, and we weren't standing under it.

I've been thinking about that first meeting. Will I be able to talk? Or maybe we'll both start jabbering at once. I can't wait to hear your voice. All this time I've been wishing for a voice to put with your words.

The movie's almost over. Singing's next. We specialize in military songs ("Halls of Montezuma," "Anchors Aweigh") and cowboy songs ("I Ride an Old Paint," "Streets of Laredo"). Victor says we'll put on a concert this spring. So while you're doing *Anything Goes,* we'll have our own musical production here.

Straight talk—You've written some really good poems, but I have to confess: My all-time favorite is "No erra, I'm your Sara." I grin like an idiot every time I read it.
—Rob

Sent: Monday, March 31 4:35PM
From: Sara4348@aol.com
To: Robcruise99@yahoo.com
Subj: The future

Dear Rob,

I didn't get to the computer until this morning. Joel and I had the 5–12 shift last night, but it was well past 1:00 when I finally got home. He wanted to talk. He's never lived outside Utah and gets really upset with what he calls "the small-town thinking around here." (I think he sees me as an outsider.)

Anyway, thanks! Your totally upbeat email was so worth getting up for. I loved the details . . . but tell me, are you a tenor, baritone, bass? I'm dying to hear your voice, too, you know.

Thanks, too, for your "worrying haiku." But I'm not trying to be another Lynn Hill. I need to get out and use my big muscles once in a while, that's all. So no more worrying haikus. The time I got hit by a baseball was lots worse than the bloodied knuckles I ended up with last week. I'd never free climb. And climbing solo is insane.

I survived the first cut, so I will be one of the Angels for *Anything Goes*. Only three rehearsals a week from now on, so juggling job/school/climbing will be easier.

Speaking of spring break, mine's over Easter, Thursday to Sunday. I've thought of going to see Angie, but I may just stay here.

Me too, Rob. The idea of meeting. Gives me shivers. The

good kind. But we won't need to talk at first. How do you talk when you're hugging someone to death? Finally, though, we'll catch our breaths and I'll stop blushing. Maybe I'll say, "My, this arch really *is* delicate, isn't it?" And then you'll stop grinning and you'll say . . .

—Sara

⟨APRIL⟩

Sent: Tuesday, April 1 3:23PM
From: Robcruise99@yahoo.com
To: Sara4348@aol.com
Subj: New plans

Sara—Just got your latest e-mail. I'm a bass, I think. In Victor's choir, we don't get too technical. And, no, we won't need to talk at first. Hugging's a better idea. More soon, but here's what I've already written.

I'm outta here on Saturday (temporarily). Victor talked to me Sunday night about a camping trip for the guys who can't go home for spring break. This was Dr. Feelgood's idea—a good one, for once. We're headed for the Lost Coast, a stretch of empty coastline south of Eureka. (I checked the Internet: great wildlife including whales, fantastic ocean, no people. Wow!)

The only bad thing is that I'll be out of touch the whole time. Nothing out there but one little store at Shelter Cove. So I'll be on the Lost Coast, whale watching, with a bad case of e-mail withdrawal.

I may have to carry some of your old notes along in my backpack.

—Rob

Sent: Tuesday, April 1 6:44PM
From: Sara4348@aol.com
To: Robcruise99@yahoo.com
Subj: Re: New plans

Not the Lost Coast with whales! A whole week? I'm so envious. I want to go, too. Doesn't Victor need a camp cook? I do gourmet mac 'n' cheese and tuna sands to die for.

No—honestly—I'm really happy you're getting another trip away from Pine Creek doing what you like most. Looks as if you've moved up in the ranks, too, to group leader or something.

Victor sounds like my dad—firm but fair. (Only Dad's more firm sometimes than fair. Hope Victor leans the other way.) Anyhow, I may decide he's okay for Ginny if he passes the Lost Coast test—and you STILL like him.

I would like to know your real name before you disappear in the California mists. Are you actually *Rob*? For all I know, you could be James Martin, although that name doesn't fit—in my mind. Or your name could even be Alex.

A week without hearing from you would be a good time to say your real name over and over . . . in hopes I'll get used to it. If it's really and truly ROB, we're home free.

To make this a fair trade, you've been emailing Sara Joy Wilcox for the last 192 days, more or less.

No April fooling . . . Sara

Sent: Thursday, April 3 3:23PM
From: Robcruise99@yahoo.com
To: Sara4348@aol.com
Subj: Straight talk

Hi, Sara Joy Wilcox. (I'm still getting used to that. For all this time, your last name was 4348.)

Good news: My name really is Rob—sort of. Bad news: My name really is Alex—sort of. (I know you'll never hear that name without thinking of Shannon's disturbed psycho.)

My birth certificate says Alexander Robertson Hayes. How's that for a handle? My father's father (he died before I was born) was named Alexander. And Robertson was my mother's maiden name. I was called Allie (Gag!) when I was little, then Alex. Up until now, you're the only one who calls me Rob.

I wanted a new name when I came to Pine Creek. Rob seemed right—part of my real name but shorter. But I didn't follow through, except on my e-mail address. (I told you about the Robinson Crusoe business. Now you know how it came to mind.)

More good news: You don't have to get used to a new name. I'm Alex at Pine Creek, but that name stays here. I'll start in the next place—wherever that might be—as Rob Hayes. (Wow, that wasn't so hard. I've been wanting to tell you this for months.)

We leave Saturday morning for the Lost Coast.

—Rob (Don't call me Alexander) Hayes, who misses you already

Sent: Thursday, April 3 6:31PM
From: Sara4348@aol.com
To: Robcruise99@yahoo.com
Subj: Hello and goodbye!

Dear Rob,

You'd never guess, but we're having our first dinner together here at my computer. With candlelight and "Getting to Know You" from *The King and I* playing. We clink glasses for a toast:

> *"To Alexander Robertson Hayes, forever Rob.*
> *And to the joys of a new life."*

We're also splitting a Subway sandwich (crab) that I picked up on the way home and a green salad I just threw together here. If there's time before rehearsal, we'll have brownies.

The email you put off so long touched my heart. I like the idea that your first name stays at Pine Creek after graduation, but someday, if you start feeling like an Alex again, tell me. It's a great name. I like it, in spite of its Shannon associations. But *Rob*, as in Rob&Sara, has a history.

Please be careful. I'll worry. Can't help it. But I'll get off an email to welcome you back. Picture me running my tail off seating folks at the IHOP. I'll picture you leading Victor's troops along the sea cliffs, singing military songs at the top of your lungs.

Happy whale watching! And come back. I'll be here waiting.

—Sara, lonesome already


```
Sent: Friday, April 4 3:23PM
From: Robcruise99@yahoo.com
To: Sara4348@aol.com
Subj: Goodbye
```
Sara—

Just got your note. Love the ending: "I'll be here waiting." It'll keep me warm on those cold, foggy nights on the Lost Coast. And don't worry about a thing. Read on for my earlier message.

Some last-minute changes here. On Sunday, Victor figured we'd have four or five guys. Now we have nine, so Bernice, our aide, will be driving another van. I like her, but the trip will be different with her along.

And I found out we probably won't see whales. The main whale migration is in January and February. So add a grandma and cut the whales. I'm still ready to go.

I'll miss you, Sara. Nine days—ouch! (We'll leave Saturday morning, probably get back late the following Saturday. No e-mail until Sunday.)

Don't worry, I won't run off. And I'll be careful. You be careful too—climbing, driving, and with Joel. (Okay, straight talk—I'm jealous of those late-night talks. I'll bet he likes you. How could he help it?) I'll miss you. I know—I already said that. Bye.

—Rob

Sent: Wednesday, April 9 8:52PM
From: Sara4348@aol.com
To: Robcruise99@yahoo.com
Subj: WHERE ARE YOU . . . NOW THAT I NEED YOU?

Dear Rob,

I do, I need you! And you're many miles and ocean cliffs away. Who can I talk to? I hate telling Ginny anything more than I have for fear she'll pull me off this job, thinking it's not safe. *(Whoa, Sara! Start at the beginning.)*

After closing time last Sunday night, I helped Joel and Brian (our 24-year-old head cook) clean up the kitchen. The servers were long gone, and Kent, the manager, had turned off the outside lights. It was 12:30 when Joel and I finally left.

We hadn't gone ten steps when we heard noises coming from where I'd parked. "Hey!" Joel shouted. Two guys were doing something to my car. Spray painting it! The big guy whirled around to run, but Joel was right on him. Caught him by the coat, then ripped it off and smashed him up against Kent's SUV.

I tackled the other one. He was skinnier, but wiry as heck. We both went down on the pavement—me screaming and him cussing. His head cracked with a sound that scared me, but he wasn't fazed and got right up. This whole time I was yelling, "That's my mom's car!" Joel was still holding the other one, arms pinned behind him, when a pickup pulled alongside us and two heavyweights rolled out. "They're gonna kill us!" was all I could think. By then Joel had blood running from his nose. He yelled for me to go back inside, but I was too busy shin-kicking and flailing with my fists.

Suddenly lights popped on. Out came Kent with a baseball bat. Lucky for us, the two linebackers from the pickup turned out to be "good guys" who'd just happened along.

But the damage was done. In big ugly letters, the entire side of my car read FAGGOT with the *T* never crossed. Minutes later, after the cops came and Kent took a look around, we found that they'd also sprayed FAGGOTVILLE across the rear of the building.

Joel kept saying he'd get the car cleaned, he'd take care of it—pay for it, all that. "No, you won't!" I insisted. We were still arguing when we got to his house. "Why should you? I have insurance." I cut the engine so we could talk. "I just don't get why anyone would do that," I said. "Why *my* car?"

Suddenly, he swung around and smacked his hand on the steering wheel. "You honestly don't know, do you? Everyone else knows! How come you haven't got the word?" Honest to God, Rob, I must be stupid. I still didn't catch on. "What word?" I yelled right back at him.

"Sara, I'm gay. They were targeting me. Me and Brian, we're both gay. Sometimes we're even seen together." I'd never heard Joel sound so fierce. "Homophobes, those guys! They hole up just outside Zion, then come in on their dirty little missions after dark. I'm on their list, Sara!"

I didn't know what to say. I wanted to put my arms around him. I wanted to comfort him—felt I should *do* something! I finally managed a feeble "It's okay with me if you're gay. It doesn't matter."

176

"Yeah, easy to say. But it matters. It damn well matters!"

By then he was staring straight ahead and I was ready to cry. I just felt so bad for him—for how hard things must have been, for how hard things might always be.

He turned away and opened the door. All I could think to say was, "Joel, wait. Let's sneak off to Arctic Circle for lunch tomorrow. Yearbook business . . . okay?"

He said "Whatever" and got out, then walked off across their pitch-black yard. I sat there a minute, staring after him. His cattle dog ran up to meet him, barking a welcome, and Joel let him jump all over him. I've never been so glad for a dog in all my life, for that beautiful, unconditional, tail-wagging love.

So that's it. We did sneak off for lunch on Monday, then talked about yearbook and everything else BUT his being gay. I guess that's how it has to be.

As far as tackling some guy in the dark is concerned, well, I did all right there. That nasty little wuss ended up with an eye swollen shut and, I hope, a massive headache. I came out of it all with a skinned knee and a bruised elbow.

I can't wait to hear from you, Rob Hayes. This week is already the longest in a very long time.

—Scrappy Sara, sappy over you

Sent: Saturday, April 12 10:33AM
From: Sara4348@aol.com
To: Robcruise99@yahoo.com
Subj: Welcome back to Camp Feelgood!

Dear Rob,

How was it? *The Lost Coast*. I love the name and can't wait for details. So how'd it go?

Sorry to have inundated you last time. Things are better

now. Joel even told me a gay joke in the bus yesterday—a good sign, I think. He seems relieved to have me know. And today he said, "Thanks for being a good friend." I knew what he meant.

Fast-breaking news: a totally unexpected climbing trip to Salt Lake over Easter! One of the guys is getting his dad to drive us up in his van Wednesday right after school. I've called Angie, will stay with her Friday night and Saturday until we leave. Can't wait to see her!

Everyone has to get back for Easter, naturally. Also, I had to promise Kent I'd be awake and smiling for the Easter-morning crunch at the IHOP. All six of us are stoked to take on our first granite climbing routes. The instructor we had here will meet us in Little Cottonwood Canyon Thursday. Friday we're on our own. (Pray the weather holds!)

Rob, I saw my first coyote! One loped right through Aunt Ginny's courtyard, almost in front of me. In broad daylight! (If you go out during the full moon when they're yipping, they'll sometimes yip right back at you.)

Anything Goes is shaping up. I'm one of Reno Sweeney's Angels, which means I'm learning to tap-dance and flirt with the sailor guys. (As is required by the play, my jealous friend. No, I'm not going to morph into Charity, my showgirl character.)

WRITE, WRITE, WRITE! We have only three email days before I leave.

Sent: Sunday, April 13 3:23PM
From: Robcruise99@yahoo.com
To: Sara4348@aol.com
Subj: Lost Coast

Hi, Sara—

Two e-mails! Great welcome-back present. I'm running them off, but have zero time to read them now. I'll answer tomorrow.

Hello, Sara. I missed you—a lot.

Great trip. Big whitecaps crashing over black rocks. Seals asleep on the beaches . . . I even saw whales—two of them at once. I almost fell off the cliff when I spotted that first spout. They kept surfacing and diving. Again and again. I yelled to the others, and the whole gang got to see them. Incredible.

Bernice was a real surprise. Tough hiker, great cook. Taught me how to build campfires in the wind. Kept the gang busy making sand castles and driftwood houses when I needed some free time.

Hard to come back to Pine Creek. Riding along in the van, I made a decision: I'm going to try to get out of here—the right way. This week I'll write to my mother and father. Keep your fingers crossed.

Right now I'm just waiting for my Internet session. I hope you wrote me a big long note.

A bad poem to kill some time:

I'm hoping for e-mails from Sara.
Her news I am dying to share-uh:
About school, play, or job,

How much she missed Rob.
Nine days is all I can bear-uh.

—Whale-watcher Rob

Sent: Monday, April 14 7:31AM
From: Sara4348@aol.com
To: Robcruise99@yahoo.com
Subj: Loved your Lost Coast report

Dear Whale-watcher . . .

Quick note: Wonderful having your news to read last night and this morning—and probably all day long behind my American history book! You did an A+ job of describing the trip. (I also love the direction you're taking. My fingers will stay crossed.)

Darn, I've missed the bus! That means I drive today. Not good because I still have remnants of a smeary "FAGGOT" on my car, which we couldn't get rid of that night. (Joel's taking it in while I'm gone, and the IHOP's paying.)

For you especially, a two-minute limerick: not good *poetically,* but fantastic *soulfully.* And then I have to jet out of here.

I know a whale watcher named Hayes,
Who's at home midst the crashing of waves.
He's doomed if he runs
Or steals cars for fun,
But may win someone's heart if he stays.

Of course I missed you—more than you know!. . . . .Sara

Sent: Monday, April 14 3:21PM
From: Robcruise99@yahoo.com
To: Sara4348@aol.com
Subj: Catching up

Sara, I want to go to Utah. Coyotes in your front yard. And you playing a tap-dancing, flirting angel. I promised not to run away, but you're making it tough.

Rotten business about the creeps painting your car. Hate and stupidity—I guess they're everywhere. Depressing.

I'm glad you didn't get hurt any worse. But, Sara, don't ever do that again. Scream. Make them run. But don't chase them. Guys like that could have guns or knives. (But now that it's over, I'm glad you beat up the little slimeball.)

Sounds like Joel has a lot of stuff to work out. Straight talk—I hate to admit it, but there's a nasty little part of me that's glad he's gay. Even straighter talk—I deleted that sentence twice, worried about what you'd think.

Here Bernice is helping the guys do research on whales, and Matt is talking about field trips for the summer. (I hope I'm long gone by then. Keep those fingers crossed.)

And you're leaving on a climbing trip. I miss you already.
—Rob
PS I helped Roland forward Shannon's note to you. I don't know what to say about it.

Sent: Sunday, April 13 9:28PM
From: Mlee1830@yahoo.com
To: Rolandjacobs123@yahoo.com
Subj: Hi from Shannon

Hi, Roland. I'm sorry I haven't written before. I know how much you like mail. Remember the time I sent you 25 e-mails so you'd stop whining about never getting any mail?

I miss you, Roland. Nobody here tells me jokes. If you have a new one, send it to me.

Do me a favor, okay? Print this message and give it to Alex. I don't know his address. And don't forget my jokes. SHANNON

Hey, Alex. I figured out how to escape from Camp Feelgood: Take a hundred pills. I don't recommend it, though. You end up with tubes down your throat.

I know how things looked, but let's get real, Alex. That wasn't a suicide scene. I'm no wimpy Juliet, and—sorry, bud—you're no Romeo. No young-love tragedy here. Just old Shannon—a little ripped—ticked off because she'd paid good money for some low-power pills.

How's this for ironic? I'm at a rehab hospital, where the therapists are after me to be honest. But they don't believe me when I tell the truth: "I was high and trying to get higher; I wasn't trying to kill myself." So I had to make up a suicide story to satisfy them.

Anyway, Alex, I wanted you to get a little reality for a change. I could just see you going on a big guilt trip, you and your fantasy Sara. (I had a funny thought: What if she turned out to be fatter than me?) Another funny thought: You could write to me sometime. I might be more fascinating on e-mail.

—Shannon


```
Sent: Tuesday, April 15 6:55AM
From: Sara4348@aol.com
To: Robcruise99@yahoo.com
Subj: The forwarded message
```

Re: Shannon—she's indestructible! Sounds like she'll soon be Queen of the Rehab Ward, just as you predicted. But like in your movie *Rashomon,* her claims may be her private truth. (Or not.) I guess we'll never know.

Your fantasy (or not), Sara

Sent: Tuesday, April 15 3:23PM
From: Robcruise99@yahoo.com
To: Sara4348@aol.com
Subj: Goodbye again

Hasta luego, Sara—

I'll miss you. Five days! Better than nine, but still way too long. I hope you have a good time. Tell Angie hi for me.

About indestructible Shannon. I never know what to do about her. I know one thing—I won't be writing back.

I liked your last limerick, but you got one thing wrong: I never stole a car for fun. All four times, it was the same deal—I was running from a place I couldn't stand to be. I took a car to get into open country, then left it when I got there. No thrill, no fun. I was scared to death. Maybe nobody else can see the difference—still wrong, still stupid, still a stolen car. But somehow it matters to me.

I'm working away on the letter to my parents. I may have Matt help me. I want to get it just right.

No wrestling video tonight. The gang is going to watch *Moby Dick,* so I'll be watching with them. Hope nobody gets seasick.

I'll miss you, Sara. (I know—I already said that. But it's still true.)

—Rob

Sent: Tuesday, April 15 8:19PM
From: Sara4348@aol.com
To: Robcruise99@yahoo.com
Subj: Tuesday night before packing

Dear Rob,

I know, I'll miss you, too! But I'll be back soon and you can tell me if you've managed to persuade your folks to set you free. *Freedom! Rob set free!* What a concept!

I have to admit, I love my freedom. I don't mean to flaunt it—honestly!—but this has been a whole new life for me, living with my aunt and being treated like "an approximate adult." (Which she calls me sometimes.) We talk about all sorts of things and she even asks my opinion.

But gloating over my own independence wasn't what I came online to do. It occurred to me today how lucky we are—you and I—that we didn't meet someone else via that poetry bulletin board. What if you'd taken up with MelodyV or I'd ended up writing to that witless Wesley? Our coyotes were definitely in alignment last September.

Better get my climbing gear in the bag and finish an assignment on *The Great Gatsby*. Will there be an email waiting when I return? (Is the sky blue? Are the Kayenta cliffs red?) Yours . . . on belay or off! Sara

Sent: Thursday, April 17 3:24PM
From: Robcruise99@yahoo.com
To: Sara4348@aol.com
Subj: My letter

Sara—

Here's the e-mail I just sent to my father. (I also ran off a copy to mail to my mother.) Maybe you'll go online at Angie's and find it. Some of the words are Matt's, but I hope the letter still sounds like me. I also hope it doesn't sound too sappy.

Dear Mom and Dad,

I've been here at Pine Creek Academy for almost a year. I've had time to think about my life—what I've done and what I hope to do in the future.

First, I'm sorry for all the pain and trouble I've caused you. I made lots of bad choices and did lots of stupid things. I know that you were trying to help me, and I know that I made it very hard for you.

Pine Creek has been good for me. I've learned to live with rules, and I've learned to work independently. But I believe it's time for me to move on.

I'm ready to live in the real world. I'd like to spend my senior year in a regular high school. I want to get a job and a driver's license and start making plans for college.

If you will help me make the move, I promise my full cooperation. I will accept any rules that you think necessary.

In one year I will be, legally, an independent adult. With your help, I would like to spend the next year becoming exactly that.

Your son,

Alex

Sent: Thursday, April 17 6:44PM
From: Angelann@tristate.net
To: Robcruise99@yahoo.com
Subj: A word from Sara's secretary

Hi, Rob! Sara just called me from her motel and said I HAD
TO tell you that she's here and having a great time. She knew
you'd be worrying your head off, but she couldn't find a computer anywhere. So it's up to me. I know she'd be mad at me if
I didn't do it, although I doubt if you're really worrying your
head off. She was in a big hurry. They'd climbed all day and
were heading for The Porcupine for dinner. I could hear someone yelling for her to get off the phone, but she added that I
was NOT!!! to start a big conversation with you. Just pass the
message on.

Sara won't be at my house until tomorrow night, so she
won't know I'm actually writing more to tell you thanks for
asking about me so often. It's been cool knowing someone you
don't even know is wondering how a person is doing. So thank
you! Doctor says it looks like I may be going into remission.
Why can't he just say, Hey, Angie, you licked it? But he won't
go that far.

If I thought I'd stumble onto an awesome cyberpal the
way you and Sara did, I'd take up poetry tomorrow. Maybe.
I'm not crazy about reading poems, let alone writing them. I
am soooo not talented in that department.

Sara's Secretary—Angie

Sent: Friday, April 18 2:47PM
From: MGGinny@aol.com
To: Gabewil@hotmail.com
CC: Robcruise99@yahoo.com
Subj: About Sara: READ NOW

Gabe, dear, Sara was hurt in a climbing accident in SLC—about an hour ago. Serious injuries, but not, I was told, life-threatening. Airlifted to University Hospital and is presently undergoing neurologic evaluation. Suspected cranial hematoma, possible spinal cord damage, other injuries. Her situation is listed as very guarded to critical.

I've just talked to your mom in Germany. She's arranging for a flight now. Your folks think it's better for you to stay in Boulder for the time being. At the moment, Sara is unconscious and in ICU, but seems to be stabilizing. Tried to call you several times, but kept getting a busy signal. I'm driving to SLC in your mom's car. Leaving in minutes.

Try not to worry. I'll call when I know more. Your aunt Ginny.

Sent: Friday, April 18 2:56PM
From: MGGinny@aol.com
To: Angelann@tristate.net
Subj: SARA/CLIMBING ACCIDENT

Angie, Major and Mrs. Meyer: I left a message on your machine. Sara has been taken to University Hospital, is presently being evaluated. In ICU now and unconscious. Knew she planned on staying with you tonight, afraid you mightn't get word. I'm driving up now, will call again on the way. Ginny Rozendal

Written on four pages torn from a University Hospital notepad

Dear Sara,

It's almost 5:00. It'll be getting light soon. You've been asleep for about an hour this time. I don't know if you'll wake up again before I have to leave, so I'd better write a note. Sorry for the wobbly writing. You're holding my other hand, and there's no way I'll let go.

Our first meeting. Not exactly sunrise at Delicate Arch. But I'm not complaining.

I told you all of this. Most of it three or four times. But you're pretty foggy. You keep saying, "Rob, are you really here?" So I'd better tell it again.

After your terrible accident, incredible luck. No, more than just luck. Miracles. When I got the e-mail from your aunt, I had to come here. I went online and checked the airline schedules, then got the whole gang together. I told them I needed to borrow every cent they had. In five minutes I had almost three hundred dollars and two ATM cards.

Victor knew something was going on, so I decided to tell him the truth. He argued with me, then said he'd cover for me if I'd promise to be back in the morning. He also told me where his bicycle was—and the combination for the lock. I slipped out and took off on the bike.

Here's the biggest miracle of all. I ride like crazy for ten miles to the Pinecrest Store—the first place with a phone. Victor gave me the number of a guy with a car who might take me to Sacramento if I offered him enough money. So I stop, race into the store to get change, and crash into Bernice, who just happened to stop for a Coke.

I just stare at her. I try to think of some kind of story, but nothing will come. And then—for the first time in years—I start to cry. She grabs me and hugs me, and I tell her about you. That's it. She drives me all the way to the Sacramento Airport (her sister lives there somewhere) and makes sure I can get a flight. She'll be there this morning to pick me up.

Another miracle: I take a taxi here and find out you're in ICU. Only family allowed. So I rush in and tell the nurse I'm your brother Gabe, and they don't even question it. They tell me I missed my aunt by three minutes. (Whew!)

Miracles everywhere. Even here. I know you're hurting, but the nurses say all the signs are good. I believe it. You're going to be all right—I just know it.

Our first meeting. And with all your bandages, I still don't know what you look like. And I don't care. I just wish I could sit here holding your hand for a long, long time.

You had the same two lines all night: "Rob, are you really here?" and "Rob, you have to go back." I promised you I would. And I'd already promised both Victor and Bernice. So I'll go. But it's hard, Sara. Really hard.

Love, Rob

Sent: **Tuesday, April 22 3:20PM**
From: Robcruise99@yahoo.com
To: Sara4348@aol.com
Subj: (No subject)

Hello, Sara—

I don't know when you'll read this. But I want to be sure you have a note when you finally come online. Bernice has been calling the hospital every day and giving me the good reports. Sounds like you'll be out soon. I hope so.

What a weird first meeting, Sara. I was so worried and so glad to be there with you that I turned into a motormouth. You may not remember any of it, but I couldn't shut up. The nurse said my talking seemed to calm you, so I had an excuse. (By the way, I think she figured out that I wasn't your brother. Nobody likes his sister that much.)

I really hated to leave. (Think about it—after all this time, we were finally together. And I had to get up and go back to Camp Feelgood.) I was hoping you'd wake up once more, but you didn't.

At the Salt Lake airport, I bought presents for the gang—bubble gum and those big plastic water guns that look like Uzis. Two things you can't get at the school store.

Bernice was waiting for me at the airport. As soon as I told her how well you were doing, she wanted to know what you looked like. She was fascinated by the idea that we'd never seen each other—not even a picture. I thought about you in all those bandages and started laughing. "She's beautiful," I said. And I meant it.

The next thing I knew, I was at the Pinecrest Store. (Bernice said I snored and smiled at the same time.) I rode the bicycle back and slipped in without being seen. The gang loved the presents, didn't care that it was their money I'd spent.

So I'm back here at Pine Creek, thinking about you there in the hospital. It was really special being with you—even for a little while. Even if you were asleep most of the time. I still don't know exactly what you look like, but I know your eyes. And I know your hand. I really know your hand—skinned knuckles and all.

I hope I hear from you soon—for all kinds of reasons. Don't worry about writing a long message. One sentence is enough. Even a short sentence.

Love, Rob

Sent: Thursday, April 24 4:43PM
From: Sara4348@aol.com
To: Robcruise99@yahoo.com
Subj: Us!

Utterly Dear Rob,

How can there be anything else on the subject line above? We were the only two people in University Hospital Friday night. I don't know when I knew it was you, maybe even before I was aware of your voice. I just remember *knowing*. And I wanted to cry, I was so happy. But you were holding my hand and you don't like crybabies, so I didn't let myself.

At first—it was so strange—I just kept slipping away. Even though I wanted to stay more than anything in the world. Oh, how I fought it! I wanted so much to stay right there holding on to you, but I'd be carried off every time, into a dream I didn't even want. (What did they *give* me?)

Then I'd wake up in a panic, afraid you'd be gone. But you stayed all night. Do you know how wonderful, how *safe* that made me feel? Still, I knew you shouldn't have come.

When I woke up, the nurse was there propping your folded

note against the water pitcher. She held it up and winked at me. (You're right, she knew.)

"You gave us quite a scare. How're you feeling this morning?"

There's no way I could tell her how I was feeling right then. 1) You'd been with me all night, talking to me and holding my hand as if it was a prized possession. 2) You were gone. Back to Camp Feelgood, I figured, as you'd promised.

And now, today, another wonderful e-letter. Did you really tell Bernice I was beautiful—in spite of bloody scrapes, a hugely bandaged head, and a spiral fracture of the tibia?

HE THINKS I'M BEAUTIFUL!

Rob, you were very fuzzy against the dim light from the hall. I could see your outline and I thought you were beautiful, too. (I remember touching your face and your hair.)

Oh, sorry! Have to move my leg. I hate this cast!

Mom's here at Angie's and is spoiling me to death. We'll leave Saturday morning to drive back to Aunt Ginny's. Angie says she's *livid* that she didn't get to meet you herself.

Love, Sara

Sent: Friday, April 25 3:23PM
From: Robcruise99@yahoo.com
To: Sara4348@aol.com
Subj: You're sounding better!

Hi, Sara—

Great to come online and find a note—especially one like that. (It's enough to make me grab Victor's bike and head for Utah again.) By the way, your memory's a little shaky. You *did* cry—more than once. And who said I don't like crybabies?

Straight talk—I'm afraid to say too much about my feelings right now. This is all new to me. I don't think I could find the right words, and I don't want to scare you away. Amazing time—the worst night of my life turning into the best night of my life. I'm still smiling.

Really glad to hear you're out of the hospital. Bernice kept getting good reports, but I was never sure they'd tell us if there was a problem.

Things are looking good here, too. I finally heard from my father—a long, long e-mail. He starts out with all this stuff about how he's glad I'm growing up—same old talk about how good Pine Creek has been for me. He can't see why I'd want to leave, and he's perfectly willing to pay my tuition for the next year. (By this time, I'm expecting a total kiss-off.)

But then he says his lawyer talked to the judge. The judge said once I finish the school year, I can go live with one of my parents. HOWEVER (Dad's favorite word). Then Dad gives about fifty reasons why I can't live with him. He's getting divorced, exploring options, unable to predict future moves—blah, blah, blah. (Sounds like he has a new girlfriend.) BUT (happy ending) if I'm sure Pine Creek isn't a better choice, he sees no reason I can't live with Mom.

Or, if I want to be on my own right away, the judge would let me join the army or navy. They'll take you at 17 if your parents will sign. (Dad will.) I'd never thought about the military. Didn't even know you could go at 17.

But I don't think I'll be going to boot camp. Mom is in her new apartment now, and she's coming to visit next Saturday. Says we need to talk about the future. So I think I'll be out of here soon. (Target day: May 16—last day of spring semester. And two days before my birthday.)

You're the #1 topic of conversation right now (beating out

whales and wrestling). The guys keep asking about you. They put up all that money, and they wanted a full report. Finally, last night at dinner, I stood up and said, "All right. I'm tired of all the questions. She's smart and funny and athletic and drop-dead beautiful. Okay?" They all laughed. Then Henry said, "What's she doing with *you*?" (Good question.)

You still haven't told me how you got hurt. It won't be easy, but I'm ready to listen when you're ready to talk.

Wish I was there/you were here/we were both somewhere together.

Love, Rob

Sent: Sunday, April 27 11:44AM
From: Sara4348@aol.com
To: Robcruise99@yahoo.com
Subj: Beginning . . . again!

Dear Rob,

If only I could write music. I'd begin with "Were I there . . . were you here . . . were we both somewhere together . . ." and the song would win a Grammy. What do you mean, you straight-talker, that you can't find the right words? You're eloquent!

Oh, Rob, I'm so glad to be back in Aunt Ginny's sunny house and back to you, who are trapped in my computer until I let you out. (Sounds like Camp Feelgood, but it isn't.) Thank you for getting me through this, for caring enough *to risk everything* by racing to my side. I'm still pinching myself. If I astound the doctors with my sprint to recovery, it will be because of you.

What a letdown about your dad! But you couldn't live with him, could you? I'm so hoping your mom will say yes—and will then follow through.

Which brings me to my latest head-butting with my mom. (Don't get me wrong. I'm VERY glad she's here.) She's insisting I fly to Heidelberg in June, then stay on and do my senior year there. I'm telling her how desperately I want to stay/graduate right here, and Aunt Ginny's on my side. More later, but I think there's a chance.

My leg's starting to quiver, but I have to tell you one more thing. A nurse had no sooner wheeled me out of the ICU last Sunday and got me settled in a room than I saw this group of coneheads pushing through the door. Whaaat?! Rob, it was Angie and the old Baldie Club, their heads wrapped in white bandages with only their eyes showing. Jessie even had streaks of "blood" all over hers. It hurt to laugh, but we all did plenty of that until the nurse got after us. Once they all unwrapped, we had to compare hair lengths. We giggled and swapped stories and passed around the raspberry smoothie Angie brought for me.

It was wonderful to see my friends. And Angie, you'll be glad to know, is getting some color back in her cheeks. "The tumor is shrinking, almost gone," she said after everyone left. I started to cry, I was so happy. Then Angie called me "a big bawl baby" . . . and we both cried.

Better wrap this up. Mom and Aunt Ginny are doing their sister act (at church) and I'm supposed to be resting. Anyway, Gabe and Dad sent roses to the hospital. And Dad called every day.

The military? Camp Feelgood all over again . . . squared!
Love, Sara
PS Upcoming feature: "How I Fell Short Rock Climbing"

Sent: Sunday, April 27 3:23PM
From: Robcruise99@yahoo.com
To: Sara4348@aol.com
Subj: Sunday talk

I came online and found your latest note   That's way too small, but you get the idea. Here's what I wrote before.

Bad news, Sara: Matt's getting fired. He's the best teacher in the place, and he's done some great work with these guys. But yesterday Dr. Feelgood told him his position will be eliminated after this semester. Budget problems.

But Matt knows the real reason. Remember Masoud, the Saudi who went on the Christmas trip with us? Matt figured Masoud should be in a normal American high school, and he told Masoud's father that. Dr. Feelgood was hoping to get Masoud's daddy to put up money for a whole new wing.

At our Saturday morning study hall, Victor told the gang about Matt. They were furious—ready to tear the place apart. "You guys want a fight?" Victor said. "Then let's fight, in a way it'll do some good."

He had them get out their laptops and write letters to their parents, telling how they felt about Matt. In the afternoon, at their Internet times, they sent off their letters—with copies to Dr. Feelgood.

Today, phone day, they all lined up to call their parents. They weren't supposed to go into detail, just to say they'd sent an e-mail. But most of them couldn't stick to the plan. They got wound up and started crying and yelling.

We'll see what happens. Victor figures he'll get fired now, but he thinks Matt has a chance. If Dr. Feelgood gets enough phone calls tomorrow, he might change his mind. I really hope Matt can come back. (I also hope I'm not here if he does.)

196

Better news: I used MapQuest yesterday. Driving time from my mother's place to St. George, Utah, is 7 hours and 38 minutes (454 miles). Wow! Think of the possibilities.

I miss you, I miss you, I miss you.

Love, your "eloquent" Rob

Sent: Monday, April 28 8:59PM
From: Sara4348@aol.com
To: Robcruise99@yahoo.com
Subj: (No subject)

Dear Rob,

No big news from here except that last night the cast of *Anything Goes* strung a neon yellow banner over our garage:

WELCOME HOME, HEAD TICKET-TAKER

I'm no longer Charity, but I have a job. The kids stayed to do graffiti all over my cast (prayerful, X-rated both). Mom was aghast, but Aunt Ginny says it means they like me.

Right now Ginny's book club (twenty ladies) is in the living room. Mom's dishing up the cherry cobbler, but I'm the designated ice cream dipper—in a few minutes, in fact.

Joel stopped by earlier. He'll be driving me back and forth to school until the doctor says I'm ready. "Only because of your hot car," he made clear when he offered. Says he'll tote my books around, too, but will be cussing under his breath because I'm so much trouble.

Okay, Rob Hayes, I figure I could do those 454 miles on crutches, but it might take me eight months. Can't you think of something easier?

Love, Sara the Pooped

Sent: Tuesday, April 29 3:24PM
From: Robcruise99@yahoo.com
To: Sara4348@aol.com
Subj: Need some company?

Hi, Sara—

Don't worry. No treks across the Mojave on crutches. I've been doing my homework. Cheap flights from LA to Las Vegas. And the Sundance Coach Company has a shuttle to St. George. So watch out, Sara: A lonesome guy may be knocking on your door pretty soon.

Straight talk—All this time I've been afraid of what would happen when we finally met. I'm no talker—you know that. I was a joke at some of the schools—Silent Sam, Mr. D&D (Deaf & Dumb), Dummy. When I first started writing to you, I spent hours on those little notes. It got easier and easier, but I didn't know how it would be when I was actually with you. And then I was there, holding your hand—and I couldn't shut up. Amazing, huh? Nobody around here would believe it.

Love, Rob

Sent: Wednesday, April 30 8:19PM
From: Sara4348@aol.com
To: Robcruise99@yahoo.com
Subj: Finally, a minute to myself

Oh, Rob, how would it be if we *could* meet somewhere? I'm crazy to see you again (actually SEE you).

Frustration hereabouts. I have to admit I'm not used to being surrounded by a mother AND an aunt, both trying to mother me. Tonight I got Mom to go off with Ginny to her Reiki class. (Whew!) Finally, time alone for my favorite "talker."

I've been thinking about your worrying if you'd be able to

talk when we met. *I* couldn't talk—remember? Did that matter? As I see it, words are only one part of it. *Touch* and *looks* are—well—just as important, aren't they? I can think of dozens of ways to say "Yeah, me too," without words.

Last night the climbing group came over bringing fudge brownies and ice cream. Kate burst into tears when she saw me, but we soon got her mopped up and set her straight about my fall. The truth is, it was *both* our faults. We were in too big a hurry, too excited, and we forgot what we thought we'd learned.

It was after lunch and the guys were still climbing "Schoolroom." The van was due in an hour. So Kate and I decided to try an easy route on the same Gate Buttress wall, but over a ways. So we hurriedly got back in harness and set up at the base. I started up with Kate belaying me from the ground.

I wanted Kate to get in a turn, so at the top I slipped the rope through a fixed anchor and yelled down that I was ready to lower off. I was about 90' up at that point. I started down feeling really bouncy about my lead. (I'd flashed it!) But what we hadn't figured was the length of the rope in relation to the length of the pitch. (Rope has to be twice as long.) And in our rush to get going, we hadn't retied the knot at her end.

Kate started out feeding rope through her belay plate in great style, holding my full weight, lowering me like a pro. I was still about twenty feet off the ground when the free end of the rope went zinging through her belay device and out of her hands. She said I arced backward off the rock, plunged onto my left leg, then was thrown over headfirst—for what turned out to be a nasty concussion.

Thank God Kate had a cell phone in her gear bag. Good old 911 had the LifeFlight helicopter on its way in minutes. I must have really scared her. Scared some other climbers, too, who rushed over on hearing her scream. I never moved, she said, never fluttered so much as an eyelid. She couldn't even tell if I was breathing.

I know, Rob, I was lucky. Really lucky. I could have ended up a paraplegic. Or dead, if my head had hit rock instead of the shaley slope it did.

I'd better read some more *Gatsby* tonight. I'm so far behind at school, I'll never catch up.

Love, Sara

‹MAY›

Sent: Thursday, May 1 3:24PM
From: Robcruise99@yahoo.com
To: Sara4348@aol.com
Subj: Waiting

Sara—Just got your long letter. Skimmed it quick. It's tough to read about the accident. It still scares me. I keep remembering you lying in that hospital bed.

Here's the good news I wrote earlier.

Hi, Sara—

Right now I'm just waiting—and hoping. My mother will be here tomorrow afternoon. She has permission to take me overnight. I don't know where we'll stay, and I don't care. In her letter, she said we'd talk about the future. That's all that counts.

Good news here, for a change: Dr. Feelgood talked to Matt. Said the school couldn't afford to lose a first-rate employee like him. Said they'd find the money somehow. Didn't mention the e-mails from the gang or the calls from ticked-off parents.

So Matt's staying. And the gang is really happy. And proud. For once, they won a fight.

Keep your fingers crossed for me.

Love, Rob

Sent: Thursday, May 1 7:38PM
From: Sara4348@aol.com
To: Robcruise99@yahoo.com
Subj. Speaking of news . . .

Dear Rob,

I wish you could call me tomorrow. I wish I didn't have to wait all the way until your Internet time on Sunday to know what your mom decides.

But good going, you and Victor (Batman and Robin)! Too bad Old Feelgood is as big a rat as ever. Some things never change.

I should wait and hear from you first, but I can't. Here's the latest: Mom, Ginny, and I stayed up and talked last night after they got home. (In the kitchen, where else?) We'd been laughing about a hilarious scene they remembered from *The Great Gatsby*. For some reason—all those sloshy good feelings, I guess—I decided to level with Mom.

I told her about you, told her everything. Aunt Ginny backed me up as to your "sterling qualities." Naturally, Mom was hurt that Ginny knew and she didn't, but I was the one who got jumped on. Mom called me a "sneak" . . . on and on . . . full-out character assault.

"I knew you'd never approve," I yelled when I got a chance, "and I was right!" I wanted to bolt out of there. She didn't know how she was making me feel. At the same time, I knew I *had* been sneaky. Suddenly I thought of you, and how it was with us that night—how a touch can be a silent "I'm right here" or an "I love you" or even an "I'm sorry." Just as suddenly, everything changed.

I jumped up, smacking my cast against the stool, and threw my arms around Mom. She started to cry. Me too. We ended up with napkins wadded up all over the kitchen island and Mom saying she'd trusted me all along, but found it hard to let me grow up so soon.

It was late by then, but somehow it had become easier to talk. If I'd spend the summer in Heidelberg, Mom said, she thought Dad might let me come back next fall. *If* Aunt Ginny was willing to have me. ("Is the Pope Catholic?" Ginny quipped.) The longer school holidays would be negotiable. Rock climbing? NO WAY! ("And we're not budging on that!")

Well . . . we'll see.

Mom flies back to Germany tomorrow morning. I wish you could pick up a phone and let me know if plans have jelled with *your* mom. My cell phone is (435) 555-1212 should you get a chance.

Love, Sara

Sent: Sunday, May 4 3:23PM
From: Robcruise99@yahoo.com
To: Sara4348@aol.com
Subj: (No subject)

Sara, I won't be living with my mother. I know you've been waiting to hear, but I just couldn't call. I'm sorry. I wish things were different.

On Friday afternoon, they sent word that Mom was at the office. I rushed over there, all excited. Then I came around the corner and saw her through the window. She was sitting straight up, holding tight to the arms of her chair. I'd seen her that way before—too many times.

Sara, I can't tell you how stupid I felt. I'd been dreaming about getting a job and a car and flying to Vegas and all the rest. But I hadn't really thought about Mom. Stupid! Stupid! Just coming here to talk about it had her on the edge.

By asking if I could live with her, I'd put her into a trap. One of those double-bind deals—no matter what you do, you're wrong. She couldn't say yes, but what kind of rotten mother would she be if she said no?

So after a minute, I put on my best smile, went in, and gave her a big hug. I showed her around the school—all the neat buildings, the gardens. Took her into my new dorm. Took her to my classroom so she could meet Matt and Bernice. Then I introduced her to Roland and Henry and the gang. (Henry said, "Your mom's a hottie, Alex!" loud enough for her to hear. She blushed, but she loved it.)

I got her some coffee, and we sat on a bench and talked. I told her that I'd changed my mind: I'd decided to stay at Pine Creek. Said I had a great teacher in Matt and some really good friends. I even told her about your accident and how the guys had raised the money for me. I could see her start to relax.

Get the picture: Me with a big smile, but wanting to scream. I wasn't sure how long I could keep it up, so I asked Bernice to have dinner with us. Good old Bernice! She took over from there. We ended up staying at her place that night, eating take-out Chinese. She got Mom talking—about her job, where she grew up, her high school days. After dinner, Mom fell asleep on the couch, and Bernice and I played gin rummy until midnight.

Mom brought me back here after taking Bernice and me out to breakfast. (We went to an IHOP in your honor.) Mom's doing okay. She's been sober 68 days—one lapse in late February. Said she was glad she'd made the trip. Said she feels much better now, knowing how happy I am at PCA.

So that's how things are, Sara. I'm sorry I got our hopes up. But, hey, look at the bright side. I only have to be here 379 more days. That's not forever.

Love, Rob

Sent: Sunday, May 4 8:59PM
From: Sara4348@aol.com
To: Robcruise99@yahoo.com
Subj: (No subject)

Dearest Rob,

I don't know what to say. I can't imagine a tougher decision, even though I know, in my heart, that you did the right
thing. You absolutely did. Still, the disappointment for both of
us is, well, huge. But I can make it through another year if you
can, especially if it means as many emails as days—give or
take a few due to hackers.

Just keep remembering, Rob—*nothing's changed between
us*. All the good stuff we imagined has merely been postponed.
That's what I'm going to believe.

You're there . . . and I'm here . . . but someday we'll be
somewhere together. (Remember? That can be our song.)

Love, Sara

Sent: Monday, May 5 3:21PM
From: Robcruise99@yahoo.com
To: Sara4348@aol.com
Subj: Good news

Hi, Sara—

Forget yesterday's downer note. It's a new day, and I
have four (count 'em) pieces of good news. I'll start with
the good and work up to the fantastic. No fair skipping
ahead.

NUMBER FOUR: Matt says I have almost enough cred-
its for my high school diploma. So I can take some online college courses next fall. "Or," Matt says, "you can just read good
books. Probably learn more."

NUMBER THREE: Let's give a cheer for Victor—the best therapist I know. Yesterday after my Internet session, he took the gang on a nature walk. Once we got past the gate, he said, "Take off, Hayes. You've been moping around all day, and I'm sick of it. Don't come back till you get rid of that loser look."

I ran up through the pines and along the ridgeline. And while I ran, I kept seeing my mother's face and how happy she was when I told her about my good teacher and my friends. And I suddenly realized I hadn't been lying to her. Those things were all true. (DUH—I'm really slow sometimes.) I thought about Matt getting me out of that mess with Shannon and Ms. F., about the guys giving me the money to go see you, about Victor and Bernice risking their jobs to help me. What more could anybody want? I came back to the dorm feeling really lucky. The gang ambushed me with the water guns. Even that was good.

NUMBER TWO: I'm quoting my favorite poet now: "Suddenly I thought of you, and how it was with us that night—how a touch can be a silent 'I'm right here' or an 'I love you.'" Okay, straight talk—ever since that night in the hospital, I've been trying to work up the courage to say, "I love you." And now I find out I've already said it. (Whew! Glad that's over!)

And now NUMBER ONE. I hope you're wondering what could be any better. And I also hope you didn't cheat and spoil the big surprise. Here goes.

Our semester ends on May 16. During the break, Victor will be taking some of us on another camping trip—to Zion National Park in Utah. That's right, Sara. The lonesome guy will be knocking on your door after all. On May 18 we'll all be camping just outside St. George—at Quail Creek State Park. And Alexander Robertson Hayes hopes to be sitting under a Joshua tree with the girl he loves.

It doesn't get any better than that.

Love, Rob

Sent: Monday, May 5 4:54PM
From: Sara4348@aol.com
To: Robcruise99@yahoo.com
Subj: HAPPY, HAPPY CINCO DE MAYO!

Dear Rob,

I'm doing Snoopy twirls over so much good news. Even my silly old crutches are twirling! Quail Creek State Park on May 18? A Sunday, perfect! I hope Aunt Ginny will get to meet you, too.

But make no erra—I'll be the one under the Joshua tree, your deliriously happy Sara.

Sudden Poetry
for Rob

From Sara, who dares to say "I love you."
(Wait and see!)
So what do you want for your
birthday—besides me?